CHRISTOPHER CARTWRIGHT

THE
HOLY
GRAIL

A SAM REILLY NOVEL

PROLOGUE

GEORGE WASHINGTON UNIVERSITY HOSPITAL, VIRGINIA— YESTERDAY

B EN GELLIE HELD his breath as the needle went into his right arm.

He exhaled, and blood ran freely into a little specimen container. It was the seventh such blood test the small team of doctors in their white coats had taken in the past twenty-four hours. The doctors had told him that they'd found something unusual and that he needed to wait until they ran more tests. Outside of that, they had ignored him.

He was tall, clean-shaven, and wore a suit and tie on most days. A junior law graduate from Harvard, he was currently interning at the State Department. With his handsome boyish good looks and thick, wavy hair, he had no trouble getting girls. It was deciding to keep them that he'd struggled with over the years. Despite his lazy, carefree lifestyle, and capricious morals, he had naturally succeeded in all aspects of his life. An A-grade student and a natural athlete, he excelled at academia and sports, and had been offered full academic and sports scholarships to study at Harvard.

Some might say he squandered it the first time round. He wouldn't, but it's all about perspective, isn't it? He'd lived like a jock-rock star—his life was about fun and picking up chicks.

After completing a bachelor of science and a semester of pre-med, he decided to turn toward pro football. In his mid-twenties, he was the NFL's first pick at the drafts. But something went wrong before the season even started. Life was good. He was moving quickly toward the goals everyone seemed to have — wealth, fame, women… if he stayed, he could have had anything he wanted.

But he didn't want any of it.

Except, maybe the women.

He broke his contract, which the media had a bit of a field day with for a while. Wherever he went, people recognized him. They asked about what happened and why he quit. He got sick of telling the story that he just didn't feel like playing the game anymore.

Things died down once the main season started, and once more he returned to the anonymous life of mere mortals.

Ben did odd jobs for a few years around the country. Nothing exciting and nothing difficult. He just wanted to get away from it all for a bit and clear his head. In the fourth year, he returned to Harvard. He was right back where he started, only this time he intended to set his sights somewhere else.

He had loftier goals than the mere creation of money.

His eyes were set on the White House. No, not as a president — he knew he was too lazy and had had too much fun in life to ever be granted such a high office. Rather, his goal was setting up a future as one of the powerful people working to develop the laws and improve the country. In many ways, a successful lawmaker had more freedom and power to do some good for the country than the president.

His recent position as an intern at the State Department was the first step in that direction, and as with everything else in his life, it was turning out just how he expected — perfect.

His mind returned to his problem at hand.

Could all of his good luck have finally caught up with him?

Ben had come in to donate blood. He'd been inspired by the motorcycle accident of a friend, who had received excellent care from the hospital. Ben had wanted to help. He reflected that, in some ways, his life had always seemed unbalanced.

Was it all just too easy?

Something was wrong with his blood results, and he was worried he was about to see the universe set things right.

At first, he'd asked questions, but the doctors merely went about their business as though he were nothing more than a guinea pig. Maybe it was some kind of bureaucratic mix-up, where everyone assumed everyone else had explained things to him.

Then, as the time went on, he became agitated and worried.

His mind raced across a number of possibilities he'd never previously given any thought to—heart disease, genetic disorders, multiple sclerosis, mental illness, and the big one, cancer.

Am I going to die?

He thought about that possibility for a moment and then dismissed it out of habit. Did cancer even show up in the blood? He didn't know. He knew very little about modern medicine, but somehow, he doubted that so many doctors would have been concerned if he had something that was going to inevitably kill him.

And why should that bother them?

They're doctors; they've been trained to treat sick and dying people. There were more than a dozen doctors. *A dozen!* Why did they look so worried?

No, they had found something else in his blood.

Something much worse.

What's worse than death?

Ben swallowed hard, refusing to let the fear take control of him. The answer came to him swiftly.

The death of millions of people.

He wasn't isolated, so if he had some horrible disease, it wasn't airborne. He wracked his mind, trying to remember any type of blood-borne disease that might infect millions of people. All he could think of was HIV, but that didn't fit the picture. There were too many resources dedicated to him, and this certainly wouldn't be the first case of HIV the hospital had seen.

Hell, any number of his friends, family, or colleagues at the State Department might have the infection, and he wouldn't have even known about it. Besides, they weren't in the eighties anymore. There wasn't as much stigma associated with HIV. With access to modern immunotherapies, people were living full lives with the disease, so there was no reason for all of the subdued panic he was seeing. But the doctors worked frantically, their faces tensed with fear.

What were they afraid of?

If he was sick, he certainly didn't feel it.

Maybe the results showed him to be a carrier of the disease, but not infected. *They had those types of diseases, didn't they?* Even that didn't make any sense. Apart from gloves, the doctors weren't wearing personal protective equipment. No masks, no impervious gowns — just their medical scrubs and nitrile gloves.

He'd watched enough movies to know that if he was indeed patient zero in some new, horrible strain of virus, he would have been quarantined in a negative airflow, sealed room, designed to keep any viruses from getting out. Anyone who came in to visit him or treat him would have been wearing a fully encapsulated hazardous material suit like the ones you see on all those disaster, end-of-the world-movies.

Ben shook his head. None of it made any sense.

He'd heard of some doctors trying to avoid telling the patient hard truths until it became unavoidable. But he couldn't even begin to imagine what they might have possibly found. He tried to imagine the worst possible case scenario, but none of those would have been out of the norm for anyone who worked in an emergency department.

The friend who had been involved in a motorcycle accident had gone out riding on a warm day in February, thinking that the roads were clear. He'd hit a patch of black ice under some trees. The hospitals in the area were running short on Ray's blood type, AB-negative—the same as his own and the rarest type. Ben did not hesitate—he came in immediately to donate his blood. Before they'd let him do that, he needed to have a blood test to make sure he didn't have any pathogens that could be spread to the next recipient. Ben had quickly signed all the forms they shoved in front of him, even though he knew it meant the needles would be next. Ben hated needles.

An hour after the tests, another doctor had come in and asked to take a second blood sample, telling him that it was a routine follow up to the first one. It wasn't long after that he was visited by a small army of doctors, none of whom would tell him what was going on.

Was he going to die?

Just what had he signed off on, anyway? He felt stupid not to have fully read the documents they had handed him to sign—he was a law graduate, after all! At the time, the legalities hadn't worried him—he simply wanted to help the hospital after what they had done for his friend.

"This is the last test," Ben told the doctors around him.

"I'm sorry, we have a few more samples that we need to take," one of the doctors standing next to him said.

She was a petite blonde woman who looked very young, with pretty blue eyes, dimples, and a soft, sweet voice. His mind instantly hated the thought of quarreling with her—but he was fed up, damn it.

"No more," he said, shuffling to the side of the recliner chair. "Not until you at least tell me what's going on."

"I'm sorry, sir." Her smile was impish and made him wish to hell he'd met her under vastly different circumstances. "My name is Emma Thompson, Doctor Thompson. I'm in charge here. It's vitally important that we take a few more samples."

"How much longer, ma'am?" he asked.

"I really can't say."

"An hour, a day, a week? What?"

She smiled again, revealing a perfect set of evenly spaced, white teeth, and a tongue ring that suggested, besides her innocent persona, she concealed something much more playful. "I really can't say, sir."

"Bullshit," Ben said, having had enough of the lies. "I know damned well that you've found something in my blood and are trying to hide it from me. When I came in here to donate blood after my friend's motorcycle accident, I asked the nurse if there was anything I could do to help. She told me I could help the hospital by donating blood because they were getting dangerously low on supply. Now I've been turned into a test subject. Last time I ever do anything altruistic. Either tell me what I have or I'm gone."

"I'm sorry, sir, we can't do that."

"Then I'm going to walk out of his hospital. And I am *never* going to donate blood again."

This didn't seem to affect any of his army of doctors in the slightest. Maybe they were used to people making protests that they didn't back up with action.

Ben Gellie wasn't that type of person.

He stood up, pushed the doctors aside, and headed for the door. He'd taken his shirt off earlier to make it easier for them to draw blood; if they didn't care about him wandering through the hallways in just his undershirt and trousers, he didn't, either.

Several hands reached for him, trying to pull him back down on the exam table. Ben just shrugged them off, knocking their hands away. His reflexes were lightning fast. Always had been. Since high school, he'd been the best at every sport he'd ever played, even without any practice.

The two biggest doctors reached for him, pushing past the ones still trying to grab his shirt.

Ben hooked an ankle behind the leg of the bigger one and pushed him into a cluster of white coats. Four people fell down like bowling pins. The other big one grabbed for him. Ben ducked under his arm and charged toward the door like a linebacker.

The doctor let out a whoosh of air as the door knocked the wind out of him, then sank down.

Ben grunted, grabbed the guy's coat and swung him to the side so he wasn't blocking the door.

"Sir!" said the pretty blonde doctor. "Please calm down. None of this is necessary."

Ben reached for the door handle.

It even started to turn.

Then someone grabbed him from behind. It was a gentle hold on his right shoulder. "I'm so sorry that we scared you," the pretty doctor said.

He turned toward her. "Apology accepted. Now let me the hell out of–"

Then he hissed through his teeth. The sweet, innocent-looking, pretty blonde doctor had just jabbed him with another needle straight into his shoulder.

She pulled the needle out and backed away quickly. A small dot of blood stained the white cloth. He turned to run. No one stepped in his way. A moment later, he felt a sudden warming sensation in his shoulder.

It rapidly spread up his arm, into his torso, down his legs, and into his head.

He blinked, trying to regain some focus. "What have you done to me?"

"We haven't done anything to harm you, Mr. Gellie," came the soft, reassuring voice. "We're here to protect you, that's all."

Ben looked directly at her. She had a kind, beautiful face. She was sexy too. "You look like a nice girl, Emma. I sure wish we met under different circumstances. I think you would have liked me." The words came out slurred, as if he'd been drinking.

The warming sensation spread into his neck. Several hands grabbed him, holding him steady.

Someone said, "Get a chair, he's going down."

"Gently, now! You don't want to hurt him." The blonde doctor said, "He's too valuable."

His knees gave out.

Ben tried to focus, but his head kept spinning. He tried to take a step, but he was no longer in control of his limbs. He tried to grit his teeth, but even his jaw failed to obey.

Someone else maneuvered his body, lifting him back onto the recliner chair. They swung his legs up, and his head gently hit the supportive backing of the recliner.

The pretty blonde face was the only sight he could still see. She smiled, apologetically. "I'm sorry. This has to be done. There was no other choice — you're too dangerous."

"Why?" he asked.

She began speaking. Something about *Bolshoi Zayatsky* — wherever the hell that was. She spoke honestly and for a moment he was certain he was about to get all the answers he desired — but couldn't seem to understand a word of them.

Instead, he felt a certain peace envelop his consciousness, before swallowing him whole.

Lights out.

CHAPTER ONE

INTERROGATION ROOM, PENTAGON, VIRGINIA

B EN GELLIE WOKE up in a new room, one that didn't look like it belonged in a hospital at all. For one thing, you expected a hospital room to have a bed in it. This one didn't. All it had was a single recliner, in which he was sitting, feet up.

Another thing you expected in a hospital room was a sink. Maybe an IV. Something that went *beep…beep* all night long. Maybe a poster on the wall saying, "Hello! My name is _____, and I am your nurse today! Please press your call button if you need anything!"

Instead, it had three blank walls, a closed door, and a pair of plastic Tuff-Ties, the kind that security used to restrain prisoners.

There were, however, more doctors.

It took a while for his head to clear enough to figure out that this was a different setting. That was probably a good thing. If that pretty blonde doc had shown up again, he might have lost it.

How did I get here?

Once he was awake enough to start asking, he did so, for all the good that it did him. None of the new doctors answered him either. They'd expanded their scope from blood tests — although they took a few more samples, just in case the dozen or so they'd already taken turned out to be duds. They took his vital signs, a chest X-ray, and a brain CT scan.

By the time the man in black showed up, Ben had given up protesting, or even asking to use the bathroom. It wasn't doing any good.

"Hello, Mr. Gellie," the man in black said.

Ben remained silent, his eyes taking him in at a glance.

He was enormous, built like someone who should have played pro football, and had a broad, blocky face, with deep-set eyes and protruding ears. "My name is Special Agent Ryan Devereaux."

Ben ignored him. It was pointless. He was going to do yet another test on him, and nothing Ben could say or do would prevent him.

"I have some questions for you."

"Great," Ben said, rolling his eyes. "I have some questions for you. Let's trade."

"I know you don't feel like cooperating. But the sooner you do, the sooner you'll be out of here."

Somehow, Ben didn't believe that. Devereaux seemed to be in his late forties and wearing a badly tailored black suit that was too small for his big frame. His voice sounded gentle but strangely accented.

"Sure," Ben said. "And the sooner you cooperate with me, the sooner I cooperate with you. That's how this works."

"I'm sorry, Mr. Gellie, but that's not how this works."

"Why am I being held prisoner here against my will?"

"We'll get to that."

"No. I'd like to know now."

Devereaux grunted. "Mr. Gellie, your eyes are an unusual color. You know what color they are?"

Ben spat out a string of curses. The guy could see what color his eyes were. They weren't shut. It wasn't like he was trying to hide the fact.

"I'm afraid that's not a color," Devereaux said when Ben had finished cursing at him.

"You tell me."

"They're violet," Devereaux said. "Mighty unusual."

"Give the man a prize," Ben said.

"Do you wear contact lenses?"

"No, why would I? I have perfect vision, and I'm not some kind of vain jerk who needs to turn their eyes different colors for every day of the week."

"So, violet's your real eye color?"

"What did I just say?" Ben asked. What, was the guy a moron or something?

"I need you to answer the question verbally. Is violet your real eye color?"

Ben sighed and rolled his eyes. "Yes. Okay? Happy? What were you going to do if I didn't answer, torture it out of me?"

Devereaux ignored his smart-ass comment and said, "Have you ever been sick?"

"Sure, whatever," Ben said. "Whatever you want to hear, that's what my answer is. Hurray! Now let me go."

"Sorry, we can't play it that way. Have you ever been sick?"

"Everyone gets sick once in a while, don't they?"

Devereaux's eyes narrowed. "Have you?"

Ben sighed. "Not really. Not ever seriously. I get a little hay fever in spring, that's all."

Devereaux cocked his dark eyebrows. "That seems a little unusual to you?"

"No. Lots of people don't get sick a lot."

His voice hardened. "You don't think it's strange that you've never been unwell?"

"It's like the question, 'How did a nice girl like you end up in a place like this?'" Ben asked. "Let me give you the classic answer. 'Just lucky, I guess.'"

"Why is that?"

"Why is what?" Ben asked.

Devereaux persisted, "Why the good luck?"

"I don't know. Genetics, that's all. Whatever it is you're after, I don't have a clue about."

Devereaux's eyebrows rose. "I find it hard to believe that a man has gone through his life without enough curiosity to ask things like, 'Why don't I ever get sick?' or 'How come I'm the only one with violet colored eyes around here?' Considering the way kids are, I'd think you'd have a chip on the shoulder about your eyes at least. Just about anything is enough to get a kid picked on. Even if he is strong and tough enough to take it."

With his unattractive, broad face, and built the way he was, Devereaux obviously knew how that worked — both standing out and standing up to the attention it brought. For a moment Ben almost felt a shred of sympathy for the guy.

Ben smiled. "I was always the biggest, strongest, and fastest kid at school. No one ever picked on me."

Devereaux laughed. "That's probably the first true thing you've said all day."

Ben remained silent.

"Despite that," Devereaux persisted. "Did you ever ask the question?"

He grinned and dodged the question. "Some of us aren't that inquisitive."

"Mr. Gellie, you'd better start talking, or some very important people are going to start getting impatient. I don't like to harass people to get them to speed up, but it's either that or start dealing with a panic. Things could get a little messy, uh?"

What was Devereaux trying to say — that they were going to torture him?

CHRISTOPHER CARTWRIGHT | 13

"What's the matter, do I have Ebola or something?" Ben asked. "Cancer? AIDS? What? What the hell is going on here? Am I some kind of carrier or something? If it's that big of a deal, why aren't you guys wearing HAZMAT suits?"

Devereaux said, "You're a special case, Mr. Gellie."

"Tell that to a judge," Ben said. "What you're doing isn't legal, and I don't have to be here. I don't know if your clever report on me mentions this, but I have a law degree from Harvard and right now work for the State Department. Once I get out, you're going to be in a world of trouble."

"Oh, is that right?"

"Yeah. I have rights."

"Let me tell you sometime about how the U.S. Government feels about the rights of its citizens," Devereaux said. "I'll try to explain why I don't have a lot of sympathy for you using that as an excuse."

"An excuse?" Ben screamed. "What the hell do you think I've done? I just donated blood for Christ's sake! And now I'm being investigated like some sort of terrorist!"

"That's right."

"Why?"

"Because you're a suspected terrorist."

Ben started laughing. It felt like he was in an episode of the *Twilight Zone*. "I'm not a terrorist, and you can't treat me like one in my own damned country! I want to make a phone call and talk to my lawyer."

The man gave him a long look of assessment. "How old are you?"

"Thirty," Ben said.

"Nah, you're just about to turn forty. We already checked."

Ben shrugged. He had always looked young—he was still getting carded in bars. He usually split the difference and told everyone he was thirty. The guy obviously had a copy of his medical records. "So what?"

"You look pretty good for a guy about to turn forty."

"Aw, thanks, but I'm not looking for a date. And how does that make me a terrorist?"

"Well, it doesn't make you a guy with a real firm grip on the truth. How are we supposed to believe anything you say? We're seeing a lot of signs that you're not who you say you are. You don't belong."

This one got to him.

His entire life, he'd felt like... he didn't know how to describe it—like an observer to the human race. He was healthier, stronger, more coordinated, and smarter than everyone he'd ever met. He didn't even seem to grow older. And his damned eyes…they made him stand out. He'd refused to wear contacts out of pride, but now he was starting to see that was a mistake. Standing out wasn't something he could afford to do. He excelled at everything he put his hand to, and it made the people around him hold him at arm's distance and treat him as a kind of freak.

He might even have a little bit of a chip on his shoulder about it. But that didn't mean this guy had the right to push his buttons.

Gritting his teeth, he said, "I was born at George Washington University Hospital. I went to Wilson High School and Harvard University. I'm not just American—I'm a *local*. You'd know that if you took five minutes to pull my records. My grandparents were born in America, my parents were born in America, I was made in America…in the back seat of a Dodge, no less. You don't get any more American than that."

Devereaux chuckled. "Oh, I don't know about that." Then, looking more serious, he said, "We have pulled your records, Mr. Gellie. And there are several holes that can't be explained."

Ben felt fear rise in his throat. It was hard to believe they knew the truth. Even after all these years, he hadn't been able to find it, so how had they? "For example?"

"Where are these parents and grandparents that you mentioned? We can't find their records. Anywhere."

Ben balled up his fists. This guy was on his last nerve. "My grandparents died years ago. And my parents died in a car crash. I was three years old. Or do you think I was forging papers at that age?"

"Mr. Gellie–"

"They spun into a telephone pole at sixty-five miles per hour, and it split their old Dodge in half. When the cops found me, I was in the back half of the car, sixty feet away from the front half and on the opposite side of the road, screaming for my blankie. My parents had been smashed like pancakes." He glared at the guy in the suit. "Go on. Tell me I'm lying."

"That's really a very sad story. Horrible in fact if it were true. But you know as well as I, that's just a lie, isn't it?" The condescension dripped from his lips with every word like thick maple syrup.

"Bullshit!"

Ben lunged forward against his restraints, fists balled and arms straining.

One of the restraints snapped.

It didn't seem to faze Devereaux, although Ben could see the medical staff getting agitated in the background. "I understand your foster parents, the Fulchers, showed you pictures of the accident."

"Yes."

They hadn't wanted to, Ben remembered, but like an idiot, he had insisted. His foster father, Mark Fulcher, had bribed someone on the police force to obtain the photos; he'd wanted to sue the Chrysler Company for not meeting safety standards on that old car. He'd known Ben's parents before they'd died — Mark and Ben's father, John, had gone to Georgetown together.

"Those pictures were faked," Devereaux said. "It was before

the digital era, so they had to do it on a lightbox with an X-Acto knife, then retake the photo. I took a magnifying glass to it. You can see the places that were touched up."

That gave him pause.

Had everything he knew about his life been a lie?

Even as he considered it, Ben knew it didn't matter. Fact was, he grew up with loving parents. It didn't matter who they were or where they'd come from. That level of love and kindness can't be faked.

"What are you talking about?" he asked ruefully.

"That accident originally happened in Missouri, Mr. Gellie. Not just outside Washington, D.C. In a couple of photos, you can see the license plates on the Dodge. They had to replace 'em. I did my homework and found the real photos of the accident in Missouri. With Missouri plates."

"You're lying!"

Ben didn't know what else to say. His head was spinning. His parents were his *parents*. His foster parents were his *real* foster parents. He'd been to visit their graves. Hell, his foster parents had taken him to his grandparents' grave site. They even made a real big show of it. Family history is important, blood lines, all that kind of stuff. There were no "holes" in his life story. None of this was real. It was all some kind of sick mistake. He started twisting his other wrist, not to escape so much as just to have something physical to resist. Otherwise, this guy's lies were going to start working their way into his head.

Devereaux said, "Your parents weren't born here. In fact, no one knows where your parents came from."

"Then what makes you so certain they were doing something illegal?"

"They weren't. Not yet, anyway. They were what we call now, sleeper cells. You know what that means?"

Ben didn't want to answer, but he found himself answering anyway. "Yeah, they're terrorists or spies who have been inserted into a specific location, where they have been integrated into the environment, normally taking on local mundane or routine jobs, until a trigger switches them to active duty. Sometimes that call might not happen for years; sometimes it might never come."

"That's right."

"So, what? You're trying to tell me my parents were part of a sleeper cell?"

Devereaux raised an eyebrow questioningly. "They could be. What do you think?"

"I think my parents died in a crash and you're lying about everything."

Devereaux shook his head. "That's one thing that definitely didn't happen."

"So where did they go?"

"You're not thinking this through, are you?"

Ben thought about it for a moment. His position. The interrogation. Everything. "You know where my parents went, don't you?"

"Yes."

Ben had to know the truth. "Where?"

"They were called up into active duty. As a result, a lot of people died."

"Where?"

"Bolshoi Zayatsky."

"Bolshoi Zayatsky?" Ben repeated the words. They meant nothing to him, yet they sounded familiar. "Where the hell's that?"

Devereaux smiled, lowered his mouth so that it was close to Ben's ear, and whispered, "Russia."

Ben grinned. "What would my parents possibly be doing in Russia?"

"They were called upon."

"To do what?"

"Something horrible. Something intended to kill a lot of people."

Ben said, "I don't believe you."

"That doesn't change the fact it happened."

"Where's the proof?"

"I'll get to that."

"Even if they were terrorists, you have no right to hold me like this. I can't be a terrorist by association."

Devereaux's mouth dropped open. His eyes widened. His smile was replaced by something close-mouthed, and almost reptilian. "Do you really believe that, Mr. Gellie?"

Ben crossed his arms defiantly. "I'm a lawyer—I know my rights."

"All bets are off, and rights go out the window in cases of national security."

"You think I'm a terrorist and a threat to national security. That's crazy."

Devereaux leveled his penetrating gaze to meet him. "That's not very convincing, especially after some of the things that your foster parents have said in the last few hours."

The second restraint popped. Now both arms were free.

"What did you do to them?" Ben asked.

Devereaux leaned forward. "I didn't do anything. But I advise you to cooperate. As I said, there are some important people involved. And when important people panic... Bad. Things. Happen."

Ben couldn't take it.

His control snapped like one of the plastic Tuff-Ties. Ben's discipline was strong, but the strain had come from an unexpected direction.

Pop.

Ben grabbed Devereaux's tie and used it to yank himself over the side of the recliner. Devereaux was pulled off-balance and landed face-first in the seat. Ben turned, placing the heel of his foot on the man's back and kicking hard. Already off balance, it knocked Devereaux onto the ground.

A pair of orderlies and a pair of doctors in long white coats waited for him, including the petite blonde. He wasn't falling for that again. He grabbed a chair from along the wall and tossed it in their direction.

The doctors both dodged, but one of the orderlies caught the metal stacking chair and turned it around, so the feet were pointing out. He looked like an amateur lion-tamer. "I don't think so."

Ben grinned. He had always had lightning-fast reflexes.

Before the orderly could attack with the chair to subdue the wild beast, Ben had pulled the chair forward by the legs, then aimed the back up toward the man's jaw, ramming the chair into it. The orderly's head slammed against the closed door, and his eyes rolled back in their sockets.

He slumped down. Ben yanked the chair away from his limp hands, and tossed it at the other orderly, who tried to block the chair with his shoulder and got in the way of the petite blonde doctor, who was taking out another syringe.

Not again!

Ben grabbed the other doctor and swung him around, stumbling, toward the petite blonde. While they were tangled up, he yanked the door open, shoving the orderly out of the way.

He almost made it.

Just as he was about to head out the door, he felt hands ball up on his shirt from behind. Devereaux. He knew it without even having to look.

Devereaux unclipped his Glock and leveled it at him. "Stop."

Ben turned his palms face upward in a placating gesture. "All right, all right."

"Good. No more games." The lines creased heavily across Devereaux's shaved head. "Next time, I swear I'm going to shoot you in both kneecaps just so I don't have to deal with this shit again."

Ben watched him lower the weapon, just a fraction.

It wasn't much, but it would have to do. He doubted he'd be given any other opportunities to escape.

He started to lower his arms slowly. Halfway down, he lunged forward with outstretched hands. Devereaux reacted fast, shifting the position of the handgun a fraction to the left. It was quick, but Ben was naturally quicker, and he'd acted first.

Devereaux squeezed the trigger as Ben's hand connected with the Glock. The shot went wide, and the weapon dropped to the floor. Devereaux's face turned to a mixture of terror and disbelief. His hooded eyes darted between the weapon and Ben, and like a computer his mind was trying to calculate the angles and positions needed to reach the handgun.

They both arrived at the same conclusion. Ben would reach the gun first.

That left a violent hand-to-hand confrontation as the only solution for Devereaux, who was much bigger and definitely more trained for such a fight. Devereaux launched a thick, heavy, fist at his face.

But Ben reacted first, as the doctors and orderlies cowered against the wall.

He twisted and ducked, then came up underneath Devereaux's hold, shoving his shoulder upward into Devereaux's chest and knocking him backward. Devereaux was big. If he hadn't been off-balance, Ben might have been in real trouble.

But already unbalanced, it was enough to send Devereaux to the floor.

Devereaux hit the ground hard, his easily 230-pound frame absorbing the injuries like a pro fighter. On the ground, his head snapped around to the side, spotting the Glock. He dived for it, expecting Ben to join the race.

Ben didn't.

Instead, he altered his position and kicked Devereaux hard in the side of his head. He was wearing a pair of heavy Zappos Wilderness boots. The heel connected with Devereaux's head with a sickening crunch.

There was more speed in it than force, and Ben assumed there wasn't enough force to kill the man. All the same, the impact knocked the giant of a man out cold.

Ben didn't wait to check on him. That was what all the doctors were there for. Instead, he bent down, picked up the handgun, a Glock 19, opened the door, and stepped into a large hallway.

He had escaped his captors into what appeared to be a large medical center. Ben knew there was more to come and that he had to move fast.

A doctor quickly aroused Devereaux.

Devereaux called after Ben. "Mr. Gellie!"

Ben turned for a split second—just to make sure the guy didn't have a second weapon. Devereaux didn't. Otherwise he would have drawn it. Ben didn't say anything, he turned to run.

Behind him, he heard Devereaux shout, "They won't let you leave this building alive."

CHAPTER TWO

G RIPPING THE HANDLE of the Glock, Ben moved at a fast run down the corridor.

There was no way he was going to make it out of a secure medical building without some kind of leverage. And right now, all he could think of was a hostage. Devereaux had made it clear that normal judicial procedures didn't apply, and Ben didn't want to go to whatever that place where suspected terrorists "disappeared."

He hit the end of the hallway and turned the corner, his boots squeaking on the tile.

Two men stepped out of an office door.

They were both dressed in civilian clothes, jeans, polo shirts, and North Face insulated jackets, but they carried themselves like military men.

One of the civilians was shorter than Ben, about six feet. The other one was a real monster, even bigger than Devereaux, about six feet four, if he had to guess, and a wall of pure muscle.

"Put the gun down!" someone shouted from behind.

"Stop that man!" called Devereaux's voice.

Ben dashed forward and grabbed the shorter of the two men by the neck. The man was fast, but not fast enough. His hands came up uselessly to try to block, well after Ben's fingers had found the side of the man's neck.

Nobody was faster than Ben, especially when he was keyed up on adrenaline like this. Soon, that adrenaline would ebb and recede, but right now, he would use it to extract every ounce of speed and strength from his system.

He pulled the man backward, knocking him off-balance and kicking him on the back of the knees as he went down. Ben turned in toward the falling man, caught him against his chest, looped an elbow around the man's neck, and then pressed his nice new Glock 19 into the side of the man's face.

It felt like the people around him were moving in slow motion.

He had another split-second before anyone else could do anything, so he put his back toward the wall, dragging his hostage with him. The big guy had turned toward him with the dumbfounded expression of a person who couldn't believe his bad luck.

Devereaux and another man in a cheap black suit had caught up with them. The other man had his handgun out, a Glock 19 to match the one that Ben had pressed against his hostage's face.

Ben shouted, "Everyone back away, or this man dies!"

"We're not looking for trouble," his hostage said.

"Yeah, neither was I. Hell, all I was just trying to do was the right thing, and now look at me."

The hostage remained silent.

Ben motioned toward the door. "Anyone in that room?"

"Yes," the man replied, mechanically. "One person. Female."

"Can the room be secured?"

The hostage paused, as though he was taking the question seriously. "Sure."

"Good."

He opened the door and pushed hard, kicking the hostage's knees out from under him. The man landed inside the office on his hands, before quickly righting himself and standing up.

A woman with stark red hair and striking emerald green eyes stared at him with dismay. "What is the meaning of this?"

Ben didn't have time for niceties. He said, "Out!"

Her eyes grew wide with incredulity. "Do you have any idea who I am?"

"No," Ben replied, firing a single warning shot at her desk. "And I don't care. Get out of here, or this man dies!"

The woman scowled. She straightened her suit and headed toward the door.

Her eyes met his hostage.

"Don't worry, he'll never make it out of the building alive," she said defiantly, as she stepped out through the door.

Ben latched the door behind her.

It appeared to be an ornamental door, made out of rich mahogany, but had two linings of lead, designed to interfere with listening devices, preventing eavesdropping. The metal latch was solid. It would be impossible to kick in, and it would take time for the marines stationed nearby to retrieve a battering ram.

It was clear that he was in a bigwig's office. It had a sofa, two chairs, and a coffee table off to the side as well as a desk and a computer and a phone. The carpet was a deep, royal blue and the desk looked like actual mahogany. One wall was lined with bookcases filled with books and hardbound document folders.

A mini-fridge in the corner caught his eye.

When was the last time he'd had anything to drink?

There wasn't a lot of time to get out of the building. "Where am I?"

His hostage replied, "This is the Secretary's office."

"What building?"

The stranger squinted through piercing blue eyes, surprise creeping in at his attacker's obvious confusion. "The Pentagon."

"The Pentagon!" Ben's eyes flashed anger. "What the hell am

I doing at the Pentagon?"

His prisoner shrugged as though the question had nothing to do with him. "I have no idea."

Ben looked around the room, searching for a way out. He wore an expression of mulish obstinacy. His focus was shifting fractionally in and out, his brows rising and falling a little, the shape of his mouth always changing, as if he was constantly thinking. As if there was a computer behind his eyes, running at full speed.

"I need to get out of here!"

"That might be difficult," his hostage pointed out pragmatically. "We're near the center of the Pentagon. Already, there must be a dozen soldiers swarming toward this office. The building's going to be on lockdown. No one's getting in or out."

Ben smiled sardonically. "Then we'd better move quickly. Because if I die, you die."

"Okay."

"Okay, what?"

"Let's both try and get out of here alive."

"That sounds good to me," Ben replied.

Ben held his breath, still trying to determine his next move.

"You want to tell me what's going on?" the hostage asked, his voice calm, almost insouciant.

It was the man with the Glock pressed against his face, asking as if he had all the time in the world to sort this out—he was just curious.

Ben knew the guy was just trying to defuse the situation, but he chose to take it as an actual question.

Maybe somebody would care.

"I came in to donate blood for a buddy who had been in a motorcycle accident, and now I'm a terrorist, apparently. They needed to do some 'tests' and all of a sudden I'm knocked out and shipped to the Pentagon. I asked for a lawyer, and they laughed at me and told me terrorists don't have rights."

Ben snapped his eyes back onto his hostage. The pawn he'd just captured was staring at him, looking him up and down. Finally, his gaze fastened onto Ben's eyes.

It felt like an intrusion. Ben gritted his teeth. "Don't get any ideas about being a hero."

"Okay."

"I have fast reflexes. Always have. And I have the gun. So just don't."

"Okay."

"I don't actually want to have to kill anyone. I'm sorry I dragged you into this, and I promise to do my best to make sure we both make it out of this unhurt. I'm not a terrorist. I was born less than five miles from here, and I've lived here my entire life. But if you try to screw me over, I'll kill you without a second thought."

"Okay."

A loud, dull WHACK of a battering ram reverberated through the reinforced door.

Ben screamed, "Do that again I'll shoot your friend in the goddamned head."

His captive remained silent.

Ben said, "You best believe I mean it."

The man shrugged. "I believe you."

The banging stopped.

He and the hostage turned toward each other again. Ben took a moment to look the guy over a little more thoroughly. He had brown, wavy hair in a short haircut that made the guy come across as a slightly modernized Christopher Reeve. Handsome, blue eyes, wry grin. He seemed almost unnaturally calm.

Ben's mind was racing, trying to think of the next thing. The next step. The phone started ringing, and he was tempted to rip the cord out and toss it. Just what he didn't need but had to expect.

"I need to get out of here," he said, trying to focus himself despite the noise.

His hostage said, "Okay."

"Okay, what?" Ben asked. It seemed like that was the only answer the guy would give unless he was asked a direct question.

"Okay...you have the gun, and you have it pointed at my chest." The man still spoke calmly. His speech was at a normal speed or maybe a little slower, just to be clear. His face hadn't turned red with a raised blood pressure, and he didn't look like he was even breathing faster.

Damn, the man could fake being calm.

The hostage said, "I was about to go on vacation, and now my life is in your hands."

"Nothing but bad luck," Ben said.

The stranger flashed him a wry, one-sided smile.

"I'm sorry you were at the wrong place at the wrong time," Ben added. "Twenty-four hours ago, a friend of mine was in a serious motorcycle accident."

"You mentioned that."

"Yeah. The docs said that the hospital's supply of his blood type was dangerously low. They *thought* they had enough, but then they gave me that puppy-dog look, you know, and I thought, hell, why not? I told him I would do anything I could to help. I expected to get dumped in a recliner with a magazine for ten minutes, then handed a glass of OJ and a donut."

"Sure."

"No. They took a sample of blood, walked off with it, and ten minutes later they were back for another sample of blood. That was not the total amount they needed, either. Just for 'tests.' I ask what's going on, and they tell me they're running a special test on my blood to make sure it won't harm the person who receives it. Okay, I've never had that happen before, but fine—

hospitals are always coming up with new ways to make life more difficult, right?"

The hostage nodded.

"This goes on for a while. More samples, more tests. Finally, I tell them that I'm done with it. I'm on my way out the door, ready or not. And not only do they try to stop me from going, but this cute blonde doc who's been smiling and flirting with me the whole time sticks something in my shoulder to knock me out. Nobody will answer my questions, but they're not talking about me being a terrorist, either."

"Go on."

"Then I wake up in another room, my wrists strapped to the arms of a chair while they take more blood samples. As if the first set of docs hadn't taken enough. Fifteen minutes after I wake up, the big agent out in the hall tells me that I'm a terrorist, I have no rights, and by the way, my parents were terrorists, too, and my entire life is a lie constructed by my foster parents."

Meanwhile, something in the back of Ben's head had finally processed the situation. He was in the Pentagon, which was across the Potomac River from Washington, D.C. proper. The entire area was a mishmash of nose-to-tail traffic. Trying to boost a car, or even a tank wasn't going to get him very far before he was bogged down. And the Potomac wasn't the kind of river on which you could just wave down a water taxi.

The answer to escaping was going to have to involve getting into the air. The Pentagon didn't have a runway — he knew that much — they flew in and out on helicopters.

But a helicopter wasn't going to take him as far as he needed to go.

If they were going to treat him like a terrorist, then he needed to get out of the country — fast. He had a passport at home, but that was the last place that he dared go at the moment. He'd have to hijack a plane up to Canada probably. And his best bet on that was to leverage his hostage into a helicopter ride from the Pentagon to Ronald Reagan Airport and to take a small jet or a plane straight north to Canada.

How angry would the Canadians be at him? Probably pretty angry. And they'd probably extradite him as soon as look at him. But it would be one more barrier between him and being thrown away forever in some hellhole prison.

Problem: he had no idea how to fly.

Solution: include that in the requirements he delivered during hostage negotiations.

Problem: he didn't want to hurt anyone.

Solution: get the hostage over on his side.

Even though his hostage clearly had the mien of a military man, he wasn't dressed for it. His skin was tanned, and he wore jeans and a white, unbranded polo shirt, with a pair of sunglasses hooked over the collar of his shirt. He looked far more the image of a "wealthy playboy" than anything even remotely military.

"Do you work here?" Ben asked.

"No."

"Then what the hell are you doing here? They don't let tourists tie up senior officials."

"I came to talk to a friend of mine."

"Yeah, who's she? Some bird you're dating?"

Another dry half-smile. "No. Her name's Margaret, and she's the Secretary of Defense."

Ben cursed. "Just what the hell have I gotten myself into? Couldn't you have been just some random businessman's son, here to bribe officials and play golf?"

"I don't play golf that often," the man admitted. "I'd just like to get back to my vacation, to be honest. I really don't care what you've done or not done. If it were up to me, I'd just let you go about your business and bid you good day."

"I'd just as soon go about my business, too," Ben said. "Unfortunately, that's not how this is going to work for either of us."

"Okay."

"Where are we, relative to the helicopter pads?" he asked.

The hostage raised an eyebrow.

"Look," Ben said. "I've never been here before, and I need to get out. You've been here before. I have no doubt about it. I'm a desperate man. Desperate men take desperate risks...like answering that damn phone and making demands for a helicopter and a pilot."

"I have a question for you."

Great, here it comes. The inevitable heroic speech. It was going to come straight out of some action movie — he had no doubt.

"Save it," Ben said. "I'm not interested in heroics. The fact is, if I don't escape, you're going to die."

The hostage ignored him and said, "Are you planning on bombing anything or anyone?"

"What? No! Of course not!" Ben was surprised and disgusted by the question. "I'm not a terrorist. Just desperate. Haven't you heard a word I've said? I'm threatening you to keep you from trying to screw me over. If I could toss the Glock and walk out of here and just go back to my *life*, I'd do it in a heartbeat."

Reilly's jaw clenched for a second. Then he grinned. "Okay."

"Okay, what?"

"I'll get you out of the building."

Not *I'll help you,* or *I'll cooperate, don't shoot,* but he was going to get Ben out of the building. All right then.

Ben started to say something sarcastic, but his throat had tightened up. He actually felt like *believing* the guy.

"Thank you," he said in a half-croak. "My name's Ben Gellie. If we survive this and I get to clear my name, I'll buy you a drink."

"I'd like that," the hostage replied.

"Me too," Ben said. "What's your name, anyway?"

"Sam Reilly."

"What were you doing here?"

"To be honest, I was just about to go on a much overdue vacation."

CHAPTER THREE

THE SECRETARY OF Defense was fuming at being expelled from her own office by a terrorist. Immediately, she started barking orders and taking command of the siege. Tom Bower stood to the side and let her rant.

The Secretary cursed and then, turning to the several soldiers who were already taking up defensive positions around her office, said, "Can someone please tell me how we let someone walk into the Pentagon with a Glock for God's sake?"

A large man with a shaved head in a dark suit answered. "I can, ma'am."

The Secretary leveled her eyes at him. "And you are?"

"Ryan Devereaux, FBI."

"What do you know, Devereaux?" she asked.

"His name is Ben Gellie," Devereaux said. "He was brought in for questioning about an hour ago regarding a case spanning more than forty years."

She raised her eyebrows. "He was being interrogated on a case that happened when he was just a child?"

"Yes, ma'am."

"Should I know about this case?" she asked.

"No, ma'am. It should have been a series of routine questions, but he freaked out and escaped."

Her eyes narrowed. "Do you want to tell me how he ended

up with a loaded handgun in my office?"

Despite his size, Devereaux shrank into the background, becoming diminutive, as though he didn't want to be seen. His confident voice softened, and he raised the palms of his hands in a gesture of apology. "I'm afraid that's my service issued weapon, ma'am."

Her face was unreadable. It was carved out of necessity. She wasn't making any further decisions on the cause of the incident. Instead, she'd filed those away to be dealt with later and was now focused on the task at hand.

Scott Williams, the director of the Pentagon Force Protection Agency, charged with maintaining the security and defense of the Pentagon, greeted her with a team of twelve heavily armed officers. "What have we got, ma'am?"

She turned to greet the director, "A single male looks like he's in his early thirties, armed with a service-issued Glock 19 handgun, has taken one of the maritime and underwater incident consultants, Sam Reilly, hostage inside my office."

"Any casualties?" Williams replied.

"No."

"Good. At least we know we have them secured. Your office, as you are aware, is heavily fortified. We can't get in, but at least we know they can't get out."

"Right," she replied. "So, what's your plan?"

"We've already got a team working to gain a visual of the room. Once we know what's going on inside, we'll set up for a breach."

Tom said, "You're going to break through the door?"

The director shook his head emphatically. "No way. That's just what he'll be expecting. Besides, a door like that might take us a week to break through. No, we'll go through the wall directly from her aide's room next door."

"All right," the Secretary said. "Just be certain when you

breach that no one takes out Sam Reilly. He's one of my best consultants, and I have no desire to replace him."

"Understood, ma'am."

CHAPTER FOUR

T HE PENTAGON IS the world's largest office building, with about 6,500,000 square feet, which houses roughly 23,000 military and civilian employees, and another 3,000 non-Defense support personnel. It has five sides, five floors above ground, two basement levels, and five ring corridors per floor with a total of 17.5 miles of corridors. It includes a five-acre central plaza, which is shaped like a pentagon and informally known as "ground zero," a nickname originating during the Cold War on the presumption that it would be targeted by the Soviet Union at the outbreak of nuclear war.

Sam Reilly quickly opened the first three drawers of the Secretary of Defense's large mahogany desk. He removed several items, searching for it, while dumping multiple pages to the side. He made a small grin as he imagined the Secretary's response when she discovered he'd been rifling through her drawers.

Maybe it was better he was being held at gunpoint.

"What are you looking for?" Ben asked, still holding the Glock toward him. "You'd better not be grabbing a weapon."

"The Secretary has the entire armed forces of the US military, CIA, FBI, and Homeland Security at her disposal. She doesn't keep a weapon in her desk!" Sam continued to search and then smiled. "Of course, given the present circumstances, I can see the flaw in that reasoning."

Ben kept the handgun pointing at him. "So what are you looking for?"

"A Stanley knife."

"So, you are getting a weapon!"

Sam shook his head emphatically. "No. I'm getting a small cutting tool."

"Don't think I can't shoot you before you get close to me," Ben warned.

Sam grinned. "I don't doubt it. You have a gun, I have a knife. You've already mentioned you have quick reflexes. Let's agree I'm not even going to bother. That way, we can both concentrate on getting out of here alive."

"Okay," Ben replied, without lowering the Glock. "So, what are you going to do with it?"

Sam opened the last drawer, finding the small cutting tool. He withdrew the blade and slid the razor-sharp blade all the way out. "You'll see."

He took six carefully measured steps forward from the desk and stopped. Sam ran his eyes across the room, mentally taking in its measurement. He dropped the Stanley knife on the dark blue carpet and returned to the desk.

Ben raised an eyebrow with incredulity. "What are you doing?"

"Measuring twice and cutting once."

"Oh, right," Ben replied, in a crisp tone that implied he understood nothing about what Sam was trying to do.

Sam counted his steps out loud, stopping at six.

Without any further assessments, he knelt down and began cutting the dark blue carpet. The result was a thin line that ran in the shape of a square.

Sam dug his fingertips into the edge and pulled back. The trapdoor opened, revealing a vertical ladder that ran into a dark tunnel below.

Ben Gellie grinned. "You've got to be kidding me."

"I'm serious."

"How did you know about this place?"

"It was a built-in secret tunnel, designed as an emergency escape route in the case of an internal disaster. Few people know of its existence."

Ben looked at him through raised eyebrows. "We're going to go down through the raised floor and just, what? Crawl our way to freedom?"

Sam grinned. "Yeah, something like that. The only trick is going to be putting the carpet back in place…"

CHAPTER FIVE

T HE TUNNEL AT the bottom of the ladder was narrow, meaning that they could only travel single file, but not tight enough to constrict their movement. The walls were made of solid concrete. The tunnel was formed by the coincidental layering of two nearby reinforced concrete piers that had been driven deep underground as part of the building's original engineering. During construction, President Franklin D. Roosevelt inspected the works and engineering drawings, noticing the natural divide being formed along each internal and external wedge of the Pentagon. The President requested the natural space to be maintained as a secret passageway out.

Sam knew about that story because his grandfather, who was good friends with then President Gerald Ford in 1975, had used the same passageway to leave the Pentagon for a secret meeting. Sam only wished that he knew the details—much of his grandfather's business involved the CIA, which required discretion and ultimately meant that a large portion of his grandfather's life was a mystery, buried by national security.

The two of them had come up inside an empty conference room. Dirty and covered in dust, Ben Gellie let out three sneezes as Sam lowered the metal plate back onto the floor.

"Been here before?" he said.

"No."

"How do you know about this place?" Ben persisted.

Sam ignored the comment. "We're still inside the building."

"That's right," Ben said. "And I still have my Glock aimed at you. So don't even think about making any funny moves."

He did, too. That particular itch that said someone was aiming a gun at him had settled in between Sam's shoulder blades and seemed as if it would never stop. Even under the flooring, in the blind dark, Gellie had seemed to know with supernatural accuracy where Sam was at every moment, no matter how quietly he moved.

And the big man had made barely a sound, even when he had to crawl through the narrow opening under the office and corridor. Overhead, the guards' boots had stamped and shifted on the tiles, while the two of them had crawled onward through the dark.

"If you're still determined to get out of here..."

"I am."

"Then we need to make it out of the building."

"Don't even think about screwing me over," Ben said.

"I have to admit that it crossed my mind a couple of times down there," Sam said. He was going through the conference room, trying to find anything that might assist in their escape. But he seemed to have run out of luck. "All I'd have had to do was accidentally hit my head on something, and they would have found us."

"Ha ha," Ben said dryly. "All right, joker, let's get a move on. Do you know where we are?"

"Yes. The outer ring of Wedge 1, Corridor 3. Once we step outside the door, we need to take a right toward the heliport entrance, which is around one of the big corners, down corridor 4, and out the big double doors to the left. Bunch of helicopters. Can't miss it."

"And a pilot?"

"Let me worry about that," Sam said.

"Everything's on high alert. We're just going to walk out of here?"

"The usual procedure is to lock down areas by wedges. They think they have us contained in the Secretary of Defense's office. Otherwise, we'd be hearing alarms and announcements outside the door."

"And if they're just setting a trap?"

"Then we duck back into the room, block the door, and head back under the floor."

"You sound more confident than you should," Ben said. He did have a point—he was still aiming the Glock in Sam's direction.

Sam opened the door. A security detail was in the process of shutting down the outer ring of wedge 1. He closed the door again. "Change of plans."

"Why? What's wrong?"

"They've extended their area of lockdown. We're going to need to get across to the next wedge through the secret escape tunnel."

Ben snarled, "So take me there!"

"All right, all right…"

Sam opened up the hatchway and climbed down. Ben followed right behind him, closing the hatch on his way down.

"Where's this going to take us out?" Ben asked in a sibilant hiss.

"The tunnels open in multiple places throughout the Pentagon," Sam replied. "I'm hoping to exit somewhere near the southwestern carpark."

"You're hoping?"

Sam shrugged. "It's not like I have a map."

"What's the point of having a secret escape tunnel that doesn't get you out of the building?" Ben asked, irritably.

"It does. Somewhere near the Potomac."

Ben asked, "So why don't you take me that way?"

Sam ignored him, stopping at a point where two tunnels intersected, where two wedges of the five-sided building met. He checked the compass on his dive watch, confirmed his position, and headed west, toward the southwestern carpark exit.

"Hey," Ben said, grabbing him by his shoulder, to face him. "I asked you a question."

Sam met his eyes, defiantly. "Yeah?"

"Why don't you take me all the way out of the building through to the Potomac?"

"Because I promised you I'd get you out of here, and you promised me that you wouldn't kill me in the process." Sam forcibly shrugged Ben's hand off his shoulder and continued walking west. "For reasons I'm quickly forgetting, I promised to get you out of here alive, and that's exactly what I intend to do."

Ben kept up at a fast walking pace. "Why not take me out to the Potomac?"

Sam stopped. He turned to face Ben and said, "It's nearly a three-mile tunnel to the external exit. Pretty soon, someone's going to realize that we're no longer inside the Secretary of Defense's office. When that happens, someone from the Pentagon Protection Force Agency will turn over the cut carpet, and when they do they'll know exactly where we've gone."

"And by that time, they'll have someone waiting for us at the exit along the Potomac," Ben replied.

"Exactly."

Ben asked, "But won't we already be trapped inside the Pentagon by going this way? I mean, surely that's the first thing the Pentagon Force Protection Agency did the second I took you hostage!"

Sam shook his head. "That's not how it works. The Pentagon's more like a small city than a building. They don't want to shut the whole thing down, even during an emergency. Instead, what they do is close down individual wedges of the

Pentagon, one at a time, concealing us inside. But we're already outside the initial wedge. Even so, we'd better move quickly."

Nearly four minutes later, Sam stopped where a vertical ladder ran through an opening in the ceiling. He didn't wait for permission. Instead, he started to climb the metal rungs, hand over hand.

"Where does this take us out?" Ben asked.

"No idea. Someone's office, somewhere near the southwestern wedge, I guess."

"Great. And if it's currently occupied?"

"Then we come back down and try our luck with the next one."

"All right."

Sam stopped at the top of the ladder and listened.

He didn't hear anything.

Sam said, "I'm going to open the hatch."

"Don't try anything stupid," Ben replied.

"I know. You've still got the gun."

"Good."

Sam opened the hatchway, thankful that it wasn't obstructed by carpet. His eyes quickly swept the new environment. It was dark, but not completely, there were small red and green lights throughout the room.

"Come on up," Sam said. "We're in the communications hub."

By the time he'd finished speaking, Ben was already up the ladder next to him. Ben raked the empty room with the barrel of his handgun, as though he were expecting attackers any moment. His eyes fixed on the only door in the room.

"Where does that lead?"

"No idea," Sam said, honestly. "I've seen the access doors to other engineering rooms, communication rooms like these, and cleaner's compartments lined on the corridors next to the bathrooms."

Ben moved close to the locked door and listened.

After a few seconds, he said, "All right, let's go."

Sam unlocked the door and went first.

Behind him, Ben hid the weapon in his trousers. "Don't forget I still have it."

As he guessed, the door opened to a long corridor that led to the men's lavatories. He walked unhurriedly, with practiced insouciance.

The big double doors that led to the southwestern entrance were completely blocked. Not by a group of armed soldiers or guards, but by a gaggle of functionaries. Clerks.

Potentially, people that Sam would recognize.

"What do you plan to do about that?" Ben asked. "Some kind of distraction?"

They had proceeded along the corridor and turned around the corner, only to have Sam grab his shoulder and spin him around, so their faces weren't visible. At least the Glock was out of view.

"Back around the corner," Sam announced. "Change of plans."

"What's wrong?"

"There are a couple of people out there who might recognize me and try to stop us to talk."

"Tell them off. Act normal."

"You don't understand. These are professional bureaucrats. They can tie you up for hours. We only have a few minutes."

"If you don't get me out of here…" The threat was clear in Ben's voice.

"I will. But we're going to have to reroute a little. Back to the other door we passed, and quick. It's not going to take much longer before they figure out what's happened."

They retreated through the casual stream of pedestrians to a door that they had passed earlier. This one led to a secluded VIP lot.

A guard at the door stopped them on their way out. "ID?"

"What, don't you recognize me?" Sam asked as he handed his ID to the guard. "I'm in and out of here all the time."

"Still gotta ask," the security officer replied, studying his face. He then turned to Ben and said, unapologetically, "You too, sir."

Ben handed him his driver's license.

The security officer's eyebrows narrowed. "He's not on the list."

"No," Sam replied. "He's with me."

The officer paused for a moment and then nodded. He'd seen Sam bring a number of people through these gates over the years—all experts in their own specialized and unique fields. "Have a good day, sir."

Sam smiled politely, "You, too."

Walking through the security doors, Sam took his keys out of his pocket and jingled them pensively. "We're parked over there."

"Over where?" Ben asked, squinting under the bright mid-morning sun.

Sam pointed toward a brutally suave black four-door with a hood ornament shaped like a winged woman—a Rolls Royce Phantom. A light dusting of snow was sprinkled on top.

Ben stopped in mid-stride. "You've got to be kidding me. What sort of asshole drives a Rolls Royce in real life?"

Sam grinned. "That would be my father."

CHAPTER SIX

T HE SECRETARY OF Defense took a seat in her subordinate's office, which she had appropriated for the extent of the siege. Someone had delivered her a hot coffee, which she sipped slowly, feeling every much as bitter as the beans inside.

She wasn't sure what to be more annoyed about. The fact that she was unable to work from her office, or that Sam Reilly had been taken hostage and depending on how that scene played out, she might need to find a new person to fill his unique role.

She reached for the report she was working on and stopped. It was in her office. That settled it — she needed to get back into that office. Her office, where she knew where all the files were, both the hard copies and the files on her computer desktop. Her office, where she only had to hit a button on the phone to be able to speak to the Oval Office.

Scott Williams, the director of the Pentagon Force Protection Agency, knocked on the door and entered without waiting for her permission.

"I'm sorry to interrupt you, ma'am."

"That's all right," she replied. "You're not the first one to do so today. What can I do for you?"

"We now have a live audio-visual feed from the inside of your office."

She stood up and asked, "What have you got?"

"That's just it, ma'am, we don't have anything."

Her voice was incredulous. "You can't see them?"

"Or hear them for that matter. It's as though they've disappeared."

"You've searched the entire office?"

"Yes. Our technician was able to manipulate the camera in a 360-degree rotation."

The Secretary swore. "Get in there now!"

"Ma'am?"

"Sam Reilly's taken him down the escape tunnel!"

CHAPTER SEVEN

S AM UNLOCKED THE car with the press of his fingers.
Ben gave an incredulous smile. "This is your car?"

"I would have brought the Ferrari, but we needed the trunk space for our luggage. You know, the luggage that my friend Tom and I were bringing on our vacation."

"Who *are* you?"

"Sam Reilly."

"No. What do you do here?"

"I offer some consultancy into maritime issues relating to national security for the Secretary of Defense."

"And you drive a Rolls Royce?"

"No. Like I said before, my dad does. I just borrow it from time to time."

"What's your dad do?"

"He owns a shipping empire."

Ben shook his head. "We're going to be spotted in two minutes."

"Afraid so. But hey, it handles like a champ. You want to try it out?"

Ben shook his head. "I think I'm going to have to keep you in the driver's seat."

"Suit yourself." Sam climbed into the driver's seat, and Ben climbed into the seat behind him. A smart move on Ben's part. Sam closed his door, pressed the start button and the thumping V12 engine roared into life. He'd wanted to knock Ben out before they got much farther — it would be easier to sort things out if the guy were unconscious and not pointing a gun at Sam's center mass — but it wasn't meant to be.

Now that Ben was sitting behind him, it was almost impossible to take him out. Geometry had never found a way to take out a guy sitting directly behind a driver. Not while that driver is moving. No way. Just not feasible. No kind of four-dimensional planning could achieve it.

In fact, once again it struck him that Ben was far more aware of the situation than he should be. It wasn't exactly a secret that it was hard to take someone out who was sitting directly behind you in a car, but it wasn't exactly common knowledge, either.

Was the guy a terrorist, or wasn't he?

Sam stared at Ben in the rear-view mirror. What he had thought at first glance in the hallway outside the Secretary's office was definitely true.

Ben Gellie had violet eyes.

It was just barely possible that that didn't mean anything. Violet eyes were rare, but not unheard of. Elizabeth Taylor had them. But they also showed up in a certain context.

The Master Builders.

An advanced civilization that had existed before *Homo sapiens* did, left some seriously strange, amazingly advanced technology behind — far more advanced than twenty-first century humanity had — and then...vanished.

A few shreds of their genetic code remained, hiding inside humanity. The Builders must have been closely related to *Homo sapiens*, in order to be able to cross with them. And it was said that they left behind a tendency toward violet eyes...

Elise, a computer whiz who worked for him, had purple eyes. As far as they could tell, she had one of the strongest genetic lines related to the ancient Master Builders. There had been others that he'd heard of, but if Ben Gellie shared the same genetics, that would make him only the second living person Sam had ever known to do so. It would also answer why his blood was so valuable—and why someone had illegally detained him.

A pair of men in white shirts and black ties walked behind the car, talking to each other. Sam waited until they were past, then slowly backed out of the parking space.

"Can we get a move on?" Ben said.

Sam smiled at the two men, who had turned to stare at the expensive car, and waved. "Smile," he said through his teeth. Then he pulled forward and drove slowly between the cars around him. This was not the best time to get into a minor fender bender.

Fortunately, the VIP lot wasn't that big, and it wasn't packed with cars the way the other visitor lots were. Soon they were at the first exit gate. Sam waved at the guard at the booth, who wasn't even looking—she was checking badges of the cars trying to get into the Pentagon, not the ones trying to get out.

Something moved behind them, catching Sam's eye. Someone was running out of the Pentagon toward them, holding a cell phone close to his face.

Sam kept driving forward slowly. He had to pass the main visitors' area and out the main gate before he could lose himself in the mess of streets around the Pentagon. Fortunately, at ten in the morning, the roads were about as clear as they would ever be during daylight hours.

Just as they were about to drive through the last gate, two metal panels rose out of the road, blocking either side of the gatehouse.

Lockdown.

Sam glanced in his review mirror, debating whether or not there was time to reverse and try to drive through one of the security fences instead. A car pulled up behind them. Short of getting out and running for it, they had no options. And even if they did, they weren't going to make it very far.

A guard started walking from car to car, very obviously holding a semi-automatic rifle in both hands as he spoke to the drivers in line.

Sam rolled down his window. The cool air nibbled at his ear, and his breath fogged up as he leaned out the window, handing out his day pass. "Good morning, sir."

The man took the day pass, casually running his eyes across the name, the face, before settling on the expensive car. He nodded. His voice curt, but respectful. "I'll just be a minute, sir."

Sam watched the man return to the guardhouse.

The guard went inside. A moment later, the metal plates were dropping back down to the road surface, and the line of cars slowly began moving through the gatehouse.

The guard watched the car drive by.

Sam wasn't concerned.

It was a Rolls Royce, after all.

He shoved his foot on the accelerator and the Rolls Royce Phantom lurched forward.

Behind them, someone shouted, "Stop that car!"

CHAPTER EIGHT

S AM ACCELERATED HARD out of the parking lot, dropping down a couple gears to manage the long and maddening series of loops and turned onto I-395 North. The traffic was light and he was able to floor it again. The plan was to get Ben Gellie across the border into Canada, but the first priority was to get out of Washington, D.C.

He braked hard and swerved toward the inside lane, avoiding a slow-moving truck.

Behind him, Ben said, "How long do you think it's going to take them to shut down the highways?"

Sam eased the Rolls Royce up to 110 miles an hour. "Not long. They'll need to mobilize a lot of police to block all of them and right now, they don't know which direction we're heading."

"There's an exit coming up," Ben said. "You should take it!"

Sam continued in the right lane, following I-395 North through Washington, D.C. "We'll need to get off the highway soon, but I want to add some distance before we do."

"You're gambling with my life here!"

Sam smiled, ruefully. "I'm gambling with both our lives."

To the west he spotted the blue and red flashing lights of emergency vehicles approaching in the distance. That meant they were still ahead of the first responders. But not for long. Up ahead, several cars started to brake. He cut out into the emergency lane and accelerated harder.

He heard Ben fasten his seatbelt. "You really are gambling with both our lives!"

Sam ignored him.

Up ahead the traffic was slowing again.

He merged to the right, taking the B2 exit, onto I-295.

At this time in the morning, it seemed unusually quiet. On the open highway, Sam released the reins and the Rolls Royce eagerly picked up its pace.

Over the next fifteen minutes, they had a clean run.

As soon as Maryland City came into view on their left the traffic began to slow dramatically. Up ahead, Sam spotted a pair of flashing emergency lights just below the 198 overpass. Ben swore. "Take this exit."

Sam swerved to the right. "I'm on it!"

The Rolls Royce raced down the exit ramp heading toward MD-198.

Sam pressed the accelerator and then stopped—because 400 yards away, the road was blocked by a single highway patrol car, parked at a 45-degree angle, effectively blocking off the entire single lane exit ramp.

Sam jammed on the brakes, coming to a momentary stop. His eyes darted between the police officer, who had already drawn his handgun, and Ben, who was sitting bolt upright in his seat next to him.

Sam could hear the tension in Ben's rapid breathing. "What do you want me to do?"

Ben pointed the Glock at his face. "Get past him!"

Sam revved the formidable V12.

The cop's eyes narrowed as he aimed the handgun right at him.

Sam gritted his teeth and jammed his foot on the accelerator.

The 412 cubic-inch, turbocharged V12 engaged, sending 563 horsepower to its rear tires, and causing the 5754.1-pound car to leap forward.

The sound of several shots being fired in rapid succession filled Sam's ears until the cop emptied his magazine.

Next to him, Ben yelled, ducking down beneath the dashboard. The bullet resistant windshield splintered into a series of small stars. Sam kept his right foot planted firmly on the floor. The heavy Rolls Royce struck the rear axle of the smaller Ford Police Interceptor SUV at thirty miles an hour, smashing it out of its way in a shard of broken glass and a splinter of sparks.

The Rolls Royce kept its momentum, scarred, but undeterred.

Behind them, the police officer reloaded a second magazine and began emptying it at them. The shots hit their target, splintering the rear window into a series of glass stars before they were finally out of range.

Sam edged the car up above 110 miles an hour.

"Now what the hell do we do?" Ben said, his voice panicked. "Now they know where we are, they'll send an army of patrol vehicles our way."

"Then we'll have to get off the road entirely."

"How?"

Sam turned off 198 and into a small side road. A sign next to him read, *General Aviation Drive, Tripton Airport.*

Ben glanced at him through incredulous eyes. "You want to hijack a plane?"

Sam shrugged. "Not at all. We couldn't do it. This close to Joint Base Andrews, we wouldn't last more than a few minutes in the air before their F16-Fighter Falcons shot us down."

"Then what are you doing?"

Sam pulled up in front of a small aviation hangar, where several helicopters were maintained for local joy flights.

A Bell 206 JetRanger was on its helipad, with the rotors turning slowly.

Sam grinned ruefully. "It looks like our ride's ready for us."

CHAPTER NINE

S AM WAVED HIS hands at the pilot. "Stop!"

The pilot, a female in her early forties glanced at him through her aviator sunglasses. Her face was set with the typical concentration and determination during takeoff. The lines around her mouth registered annoyance, more than concern. She raised both her palms skyward and mouthed the words, "What is it?"

Having stopped her from taking off, Sam didn't wait. He moved in quickly and opened her side door. "I'm sorry, ma'am. You're needed back at the office."

Sam saw her look over the two of them with a single, contemptuous glance.

"What's the problem?"

Sam had to shout to be heard. "We need you to go back to the main office. There's a problem with the flight plan that you filed."

"No there isn't," she said. "We're a charter service that stays out of D.C.'s no fly zone. I'm running some routine maintenance tests without any passengers, so I don't have to lodge any flight plans."

"Yes," he said, emphatically, looking at the hilt of the handgun sticking prominently out of Ben's belt. "There is."

Her eyes widened as she noticed the bulge sticking out of the front of Ben's pocket. Her mouth tightened. "Okay!" she shouted. "I'll get right on that."

She reached into the JetRanger to shut down the engine. Sam grabbed her wrist first, gripping it hard, and twisting it so that she couldn't disengage the engine.

He said, "That's not necessary. This is going to be quick. Just move out of the area, please, ma'am."

"They're waving at you," she said, trying to keep her voice low, but still having to shout.

"I know," he grinned through gritted teeth. "I just wanted to go on a vacation. Plans change."

"What?" she said.

"Never mind."

She nodded and walked past him. Sam turned to watch her go. She passed Ben without incident, not even looking his way.

Sam said, "Get in."

Ben pointed the Glock at him. "You first."

Sam nodded and climbed up into the pilot's chair. He buckled his harness and put on a pair of headphones. He ran his eyes across the series of instruments, taking their values in with a glance. The helicopter was full of fuel and it was ready to take-off.

Ben came around the opposite side of the cockpit and climbed in, closing the door behind him. Sam handed him a set of headphones. Ben closed the door and latched it.

His hand wavered for a second on the cyclic control. A moment later, he increased the throttle and the engine whined as its RPM increased to 95 percent of its maximum speed. The blades above thudded, drowning out all external sound. Sam placed his feet on the antitorque pedals, applying the slightest of pressure. His right hand adeptly gripped the cyclic control.

In the distance were some flashing red and blue lights, heading toward them.

Sam held the collective control, which looked similar to a handbrake in a car, and pulled it upward. The powerful JetRanger threw off the chains of gravity and took off into the air. He performed the delicate balancing act, managing the pedals, cyclic control, and collective. At an altitude of fifty feet, he dropped the nose downward, and headed off due north.

He grinned.

Everything was going to be all right.

CHAPTER TEN

THE SECRETARY OF Defense sat at her recently appropriated desk, where she checked and signed off a series of routine reports. Her eyes glanced over a message regarding the search and rescue of the *USS Omega Deep* and leveled at a single statement she'd written by hand no more than a couple hours earlier during her debrief with Sam Reilly — *There is a traitor in the Pentagon.*

For a moment, she wondered if there could be a connection to the hostage situation and the traitor. She made a mental note to find out more about the man who had taken Sam Reilly hostage. So far, she knew that the man had been taken in for questioning regarding something his parents had done during the seventies and had been told that the man had gone crazy and broke out of the interrogation room, stealing an FBI agent's handgun in the process. She had searched the standard array of databases at her disposal but found little of interest on file about the man, and nothing about his parents.

Who are you Ben Gellie?

There was no doubt in her mind that someone was lying to her about his background. The question still remained in her mind, *Who?*

She made a defiant decision to find out.

Her next train of thought was interrupted by a curt knock at her door.

The Secretary looked up to see Scott Williams, the director of the Pentagon Protection Force Agency waiting.

"I'm sorry to interrupt, ma'am."

"What did you find?" she asked without preamble.

"We've located Sam Reilly and Ben Gellie."

"Where?"

"Tripton Airport, Maryland."

The Secretary stood up. "The airport. What does he expect to do there, hijack a plane?"

"He's just stolen a JetRanger."

"A helicopter?" The Secretary of Defense made a wry smile. "Where the hell does he think he's going to get in that?"

"Beats me," Williams replied. "F16s have already been scrambled from Joint Andrews Airforce Base."

The Secretary set her jaw. Turning to her aide, she said, "Get me the commander of the 113th Wing, D.C. Air National Guard at Joint Base Andrews on the line. I want to make myself emphatically clear, one of my best consultants is on board that helicopter, and unless it's about to fly into the White House I don't authorize anyone to shoot it down!"

"Understood ma'am."

The Secretary picked up a phone on her desk and dialed a number by heart.

A woman's voice answered on the first ring. "12th Aviation Battalion."

"This is the Secretary of Defense. I'm on my way up; I need a helicopter ready to go right now!"

"Yes ma'am," came the immediate response.

The Secretary of Defense stood up.

Director Williams asked, "Where are you going?"

"To catch up with that JetRanger. Someone's doing something they're not telling me about. I want to make sure that I get there before someone does something really stupid."

"That's really not necessary…"

She gave a curt wave of her hand to stop him. "I'm afraid it is. Someone's lying to me. I want eyes on that target when the F16s intercept it."

"Understood ma'am."

She turned to Tom, who was waiting just outside her makeshift office. "Mr. Bower, you can come too. Maybe you can tell me why it appears Sam Reilly is helping this man escape."

Tom turned and raised his hands in supplication. "You know as much as I do, ma'am."

She set her cold, piercing eyes hard on him. "We'll see. We'll see."

CHAPTER ELEVEN

B EN GELLIE FORCED himself to relax into the helicopter seat.
He was terrified of flying and, if the news was anything
to go by, helicopters held the worst safety record for forms of
flight. As far as he was concerned the damned things went
against the fundamental laws of physics. Not that he had a
choice at the moment.

He expelled a deep breath of air, his heart still thumping hard
in his chest. He mentally searched a map of the eastern seaboard.
If they flew in a beeline, the closest Canadian border would see
them in Toronto in a little less than 500 miles.

It might as well be the moon given their current location.

Below him were the flashing red and blue lights of the local
highway patrol.

Already, they would be radioing their base to report the theft
of the helicopter. It wouldn't take long for someone to make the
connection with the Rolls Royce and the helicopter and
determine that the helicopter was stolen by Sam Reilly. Ben
Gellie had little understanding about the system of airways
across the eastern seaboard, but given their close proximity to
Washington, D.C. it wasn't hard to guess that someone would
locate the JetRanger on radar pretty quickly.

Then it would be a matter of determining their level of threat.

Would they shoot them down or force them to land? If so, how long
would it take the local F16 Falcons to be in the air and in a

position to shoot them down? He didn't have to search far for the answer to that question: not very long. Would they wait until they had cleared the heavily populated cities? If they landed, could they escape on the ground? The answer came back as a resounding no.

The crisp air was unusually cold for early spring. There was a gibbous moon with no cloud cover whatsoever. With the helicopter flying in a nose down position, Ben stared through the windshield. The night's canvas of velvet darkness was intermittently broken by the sparkle of a handful of stars struggling to compete for exposure against the radiant glow of Washington, D.C. Slow moving red and green lights zigzagged across the horizon, indicating routine air traffic for the region. A mixture of commercial jets, private helicopters, and military aircraft.

His eyes darted to the ground below.

Already, he could make out the series of flashing blue and red lights across the highway, where police continued to check the roadblock. They were still searching for him. It was a good sign. If the roadblocks had been opened, he would have known for certain that they knew he was in the helicopter.

Right now, someone would be reporting the hijacking of the helicopter to the police, who would be reporting it to Ronald Reagan Airport's air traffic control, who would in turn be searching their radar screens for the stolen helicopter. Despite their advanced systems, Ben hoped that it was harder said than done to pinpoint an individual helicopter out of a sea of commercial traffic.

It would be given a high priority, but much lower than had a commercial jet been hijacked. The helicopter was small and light with no inbuilt weapons bar its weight to be used in a terrorist attack.

They would be deemed a low risk.

Until someone realized that he was on board.

He swallowed hard.

There was no doubt in his mind the F16s from Joint Base Andrews would be scrambled as soon as the connection had been made.

He turned his eyes to the right, leveling them at his captive, Sam Reilly. Despite the man's obvious wealth, he flew with the comfort of a professional who'd spent years piloting a helicopter. The man was adeptly maneuvering the complex set of controls, flying the aircraft very low.

Ben asked, "Any idea how long the flight to the border is going to be?"

"No idea," Sam replied without looking at him. "Why, were you planning on trying to fly to the Canadian border?"

Ben's right hand tentatively touched the Glock's hilt, reassuring him that he still had the weapon. He didn't take it out from where he'd tucked it into his belt earlier. There was no need to wave it around now that they were in the air. They were at an impasse. He had no idea how to fly a helicopter, so he couldn't kill Sam and Sam had no reason to land anywhere other than where Ben wanted because he still held the gun.

Ben let himself smile. "You heard the Secretary of Defense. The DoD won't spare a dime over this. They'll launch the largest fugitive hunt since 9/11 and they won't stop until they catch me."

"You think they're going to stop when you reach Canada?"

Ben swallowed hard. "You're right. They have an extradition treaty, but Canada's not about to let thousands of FBI agents in to scour their countryside. Ideally, I'd head south, across the border, but we both know that's an impossible journey for me to make. You got a better idea?"

Sam said, "As a matter of fact, I do."

CHAPTER TWELVE

T HE JETRANGER DROPPED suddenly.
With its nose dipped in a downward attitude, the helicopter raced toward the ground some hundred feet below, before leveling out just above the blacktop of a maple tree lined road into Hagerstown. Ben held his breath, gripping the side of his seat until his knuckles turned white. Above him, he watched the haze of spinning rotor blades overhead running dangerously close to the foliage of the row of maple trees that seemed to continually encroach farther across the roadway.

Sam shoved the cyclic control—the joystick like device between his legs—to the left and the helicopter banked south, swinging round like the cart of a rollercoaster. Ben felt blood rush to the back of his head as he swung round the sharp bend.

He wanted to scream and tell Sam to stop but was too terrified that any distraction might just cause the man to crash and kill them both.

The helicopter seemed to speed up—if that was possible.

At 2 a.m. the roads were empty. Sam flew along the road; the helicopter's skids were no more than a foot off the ground.

Up ahead, the three-lane highway lit up with the powerful lights of an oncoming Mac truck.

Ben shouted, "Truck! Truck!"

Sam remained silent. His gaze fixed straight ahead, controlling the helicopter with infinitesimal precision movements as they raced toward certain death. Ben noticed with abject horror that the man's face was still plastered with unshakable insouciance.

Did the man want to die?

Ben felt the thump of his heart pounding in his chest, as he realized the greater possibility that the man had mentally snapped.

Was he trying to kill them?

"For God's sake!" Ben shouted. "The truck's going to hit us!"

The truck jammed on its brakes, sending a bluish rubber filled smoke from its tires.

Ben's eyes darted between the truck and the ornamental arbor of maple trees that enveloped the roadway.

Was there even enough room to ascend, or would the rotor blades hit the branches? Which way would Sam go? Ben gritted his teeth.

The maple trees disappeared as the road approached the Williamsport Bridge crossing the Potomac.

Sam threw the controls hard to the left. The helicopter banked along an invisible razorblade sharp bend as though it were on rails, going over the edge of the bridge, before dropping down sharply over the guardrails.

Ben felt his head snap round with the sudden, jarring movement.

An instant later, Sam brought the helicopter back to straight and level—no more than a foot off the river.

Behind them, the prolonged honk of the truck disappeared with the Doppler effect.

Sam turned his head to meet his eye. "I'm sorry. What did you say?"

Ben expelled a deep breath and forced his clenched hands to

open. "You want to tell me why you felt the need to nearly get us killed?"

Sam shrugged. "We're still alive, aren't we?"

"All the same, I'd like to know why you felt the need to try and kill us."

"To confuse the professional guys and gals at Potomac TRACON."

Ben stared at him, his face vacant. "What?"

Sam closed his eyes for a split second, his jaw set in a half-lipped smile, as though he was trying to decide where to start. "What do you think of when you think of air traffic control?"

"The little glass tower at the end of the runway."

"Right. Most people do. Those people in the tower, they're called tower controllers. They guide an aircraft from the terminal to the runway, and manage their take-offs and descent approaches up until about five miles from the airport."

"Okay," Ben said, impatient for him to get to the point. "So what?"

"So, the rest of the time, which happens to be the majority of it, the aircraft is tracked by a dedicated team of men and women from the Terminal Radar Approach Controllers. Although they don't know it yet, we're currently being tracked by TRACON at Potomac."

"They don't know they're tracking us?"

Sam shook his head. "They know we're here, but they don't care. They're more concerned with aircraft flying at high altitude. They're not interested in a helicopter flying less than a hundred feet off the ground."

"But they're tracking us anyway?"

Sam dipped the helicopter, following the Potomac River due south, keeping the helicopter's skids just above the water, like a pair of water skis.

He exhaled a deep breath of air, his eyes set on the horizon ahead. "Any minute now, those highway patrol officers are going to report the theft of the helicopter and TRACON will be tasked with the job of locating us. They'll go through their data recordings to follow us from our very takeoff at Tripton Airport to our GPS location near Hagerstown."

"So, there's nothing we can do about it?"

The edges of Sam cheeks were lined with the evidence of a prominent grin. It imbued confidence, like a man used to winning. "Sure, there is. We just crossed the border."

Ben let the words hang there for a moment in silence. "Is that supposed to mean something to me?"

"The Williamsport Bridge is the edge of the Potomac TRACON's region. After that the area blends with Cleveland, Ohio's TRACON. But Cleveland's TRACON haven't been tasked to look for a helicopter."

"Which means... what? They've lost us?"

Sam nodded. "At that point, I dropped our altitude low enough that neither TRACON could have followed our movements."

Ben grinned. "Last they will see we're flying south out of Hagerstown and now we're racing along the Potomac."

"That's the idea."

"How long will the ruse last?"

Sam said, "Both TRACONs will assume we were being watched by the other. When someone eventually tracks back, they'll discover we disappeared off the radar and presumably crashed. Or landed."

"How long will that last?"

"I have no idea. I've never tried to deceive our own dedicated men and women before."

Despite the tension in the air, Sam wore a carefree grin and his piercing blue eyes were wide with pleasure as he raced along the surface of the river.

Ben stared at him through slightly raised eyebrows. "You're enjoying this, aren't you?"

Sam shrugged without turning his head. "It's okay. I didn't set out to be taken hostage today, but hey, as far as abductors go, you seem like a pretty good guy."

Ben laughed. "If it makes you feel better, I didn't set out to take any hostages today, but as far as prisoner's go, you seem like a pretty decent guy yourself."

Sam nodded, but remained silent.

Up ahead a large concrete bridge crossed the river. Sam increased their altitude, before banking right, and settling the JetRanger into straight and level just above the blacktop on I-81 south. Once there, Sam increased the speed, racing along the highway at 110 miles per hour.

Ben asked, "What are you doing?"

"Radar won't follow us along the highway. Even if they could spot us, their computers would assume we're a small truck, not a helicopter."

"Obviously the people driving here are going to take notice."

"Sure, they will, but that won't matter. They'll tune into their radios to see if there's an accident up ahead or something, but it's unlikely they're going to call 911 over it. Eventually, someone will post it to their social media feeds, and the game's up, but by then, hopefully we'll be long gone."

"You're serious, aren't you?"

Sam nodded. "Sure, why not?"

Ben curled his lips upward into a grin. "You're crazy."

CHAPTER THIRTEEN

THE JETRANGER RACED south along I-81.

After the helicopter's swift movements, it now felt almost stationary as it hovered above the highway at more than a hundred miles an hour. Even the best cars allowed some small bumps, sudden movements, into the cabin on the highway, but as the helicopter hovered, it was perfectly smooth.

Ben listened to the constant drone of the rotor blades above; his eyes followed the yellow broken lines that marked the edge of the road, as they appeared to blend into one constant unbroken line, with speed.

He closed his eyes. Resting, but not sleeping.

Drifting in and out of focus, in a transient state—not really awake—he opened his eyes and looked at Sam. The man's jaw was set, his eyes focused, but he wore the casual indifference of a driver heading out on a vacation.

Ben said, "You mentioned before that you had a theory why the FBI thinks I'm a terrorist?"

Sam nodded. "I do, but they're not really worried about you being a terrorist."

"That's great to know," Ben said drily. "What do they think I am then, a Girl Scout?"

"They think you're a descendent of an ancient race known as Master Builders."

"A what?"

Sam met his eye. He paused and expelled a deep breath, as though not really sure how much to say or even where to begin. "Have you ever wondered how the ancient Egyptians built the pyramids?"

"No."

"Really?" Sam looked at him through raised eyebrows. His face painted with incredulity.

Ben shrugged his broad shoulders. "I've never really had any interest in all that archeology stuff. I'm more a present time kind of guy. Let the past be the past."

Sam opened his mouth, ready to put up an argument about the importance of learning from the past, and then closed it again. He swung the helicopter around an 18-wheeler truck with a deft movement of the cyclic collective to the right, before straightening up again.

Ben felt his heart thumping away in his chest. "What about the pyramids?"

"Have you ever been to Egypt and stood at the base of the Pyramid of Giza?"

"No, but I went to school. I've seen photos."

Sam scrunched his face as though the comment physically hurt him. "It's not the same."

Ben didn't miss a beat. "What about the pyramids?"

"Do you honestly think a four-thousand-year old civilization could have built something like that using technologies that predated the invention of the wheel?"

Ben shrugged. "I haven't given it a thought at all."

"What's wrong with you?" Sam asked. "Every kid in the world who's seen a photo of the Great Pyramid has asked the question—how on Earth did they build it?"

"Yeah, well not me. Like I said, let the past be in the past."

Sam started, "Just imagine..."

"I get the idea. The pyramids are big. I've heard all the stories before. It's an amazing feat, but somehow, they managed it."

"No, you don't get the idea!" Sam said, without breaking stride. "The Great Pyramid consists of an estimated 2.3 million blocks which most believe to have been transported from nearby quarries. The Tura limestone used for the casing was quarried across the river. The largest granite stones in the pyramid, found in the King's chamber weighed between 50 and 80 tons and were transported from Aswan, more than 500 miles away. It is estimated that 5.5 million tons of limestone, 8,000 tons of granite, and 500,000 tons of mortar were used in the construction of the Great Pyramid."

"Okay, so they're really big!"

Sam continued. "The tombs are aligned north-south with an accuracy of up to 0.05 degrees. Today, you could align a building north-south by pointing the sides towards the pole star, which sits roughly at true north. The mortar used is stronger than the stone used to build the pyramid and is still in place today. Despite modern science, no one has been able to reverse engineer the mortar."

"So," Sam concluded, "now do you want to throw a guess at how the ancient Egyptians achieved such an extraordinary feat?"

"Didn't the guards have really big whips or something?"

"Actually," Sam intervened. "Archeological evidence suggests the ancient Egyptians used skilled laborers, paid for their service, and not slaves."

Ben shrugged. "Okay, what's this got to do with the FBI trying to take my life away?"

Sam continued without breaking stride. "Have you ever wondered if we could build the same structure using modern technologies?"

"No. But I assume we could."

"The answer is we're still not capable of it. Each of those

blocks weighs as much as 15 tons. To place one at the top of the 481-foot pyramid would be impossible. Yet, each block is so perfectly positioned that not even a hair could be slid through it."

"Okay, so how did they do it?"

"They didn't."

"Who did then?"

"The Master Builders."

"What, like aliens?" Ben laughed, and then noticing Sam was serious, said, "Okay, so how did they do it?"

"No one knows, but if a civilization that lived more than 4000 years ago had technologies superior to ours today, we want to know about it. And if their knowledge is still out there, then the U.S. military perceives that as a threat."

Ben opened his mouth to speak, closed his eyes and shook his head in dismissal. "They think I'm an ancient engineer?"

"That's my guess."

"And they're afraid of my potential engineering ability because they're worried I might make a weapon that will kill everyone?"

Sam nodded. "It's just a guess."

"I don't even like science and math, let alone engineering. And as for building a weapon that's capable of being a threat to the US, I don't even own a gun." Ben gripped the Glock in his hand and folded his hands across his lap. "Except this one, but I assure you my ownership will be short lived. I'll get rid of it as soon as I get out of this mess."

Sam let those words sit in silence for a while.

The helicopter raced by for a few more minutes in silence before Ben broke it.

He asked, "Why do they think I'm a Master Builder?"

Sam said, "For starters, you have purple eyes."

"So did Elizabeth Taylor, but I don't see anyone locking her up for life."

"You had bloods taken."

"And what did they show?"

"I have no idea. Maybe there's a genetic trait. An ancient marker."

"So they think I share DNA with ancient engineers," Ben asked through narrowed eyes. "I hated science at school and struggled with math. I mean I got it, but it didn't come naturally to me either."

Sam took the helicopter up a notch to clear a bridge, before quickly descending again. "Not everything's genetic, I guess. How were the rest of your grades?"

Ben had been at the top of every educational institution he'd ever been part of. "I did okay."

Sam lifted his eyebrows. "So some things were passed down."

Ben nodded his agreement. "Maybe. The rest of it makes sense."

"Really?"

"Yeah. The questions they were asking at the Pentagon make more sense now."

Sam grinned. "What sort of questions?"

"Had I ever been sick, more than a sniffle? Had I ever been seriously injured? How was my memory? Did I have to work hard to memorize facts and figures?"

Sam added, "Why are your eyes violet?"

Ben's lips curled into a half-smile. "Yeah. They did ask that. At the time I thought they were just trying to irritate me, you know, get under my skin, but there's a connection, isn't there?"

"Eye color seems to be a dominant gene in Master Builders. Not that we have a lot of living ones to go off."

"That's good to know," Ben said. "So they're taking this little bit of nothing and turning it into a witch hunt."

"Yes. But we're running out of time. People are starting to panic."

Ben's eyes narrowed. "Why?"

"Some believe the descendants of the Master Builders are working toward a coordinated attack on governments around the world."

"World War III?"

"No," Sam replied, shaking his head. "Think of it as more of an insurrection. Master Builders will infiltrate all levels of government in countries around the world."

"For what purpose?"

"We don't know that either. But it's a frightening thought, isn't it? A group of highly intelligent people, capable of dominating entire civilizations thousands of years ago. What could they achieve once they gained control of modern government?"

"Yeah, that's a scary thought." Ben grimaced. "So it's to be guilt by ancient DNA."

"Looks like it. Either that, or this has nothing to do with Master Builders and you really are a terrorist planning a deadly attack."

Ben opened his mouth to defend himself. Instead, he cursed loudly.

Because a highway patrol car had just spotted them.

CHAPTER FOURTEEN

S AM PULLED BACK on the collective, sending the JetRanger into a steep climb. At a hundred feet, he jammed his right foot on the antitorque pedal, dipped the collective, and swung round in a wide arc, finishing in an easterly direction.

"Where are you going?" Ben asked.

"That highway patrol officer is going to report our location. We need to be somewhere else before they can scramble any fighter jets to greet us."

Ten minutes later, Sam zigzagged into a southwestern direction again, keeping the helicopter down low.

Ben glanced over his shoulder. "Hey, it looks like you lost him!"

"Of course we lost him!" Sam replied. "He's in a car and we're in a helicopter. The trouble's going to be keeping hidden from the fighter squadron that I have no doubt is currently being scrambled to find us."

Ben swallowed. "What's your plan?"

"I don't have a plan. This is your show remember?"

"I thought you said you believed me. I'm innocent!"

"I never said I thought you were innocent, but I had a fair idea why they're after you despite you having never done a thing wrong in your life."

"Hey, that is innocent!" Ben protested.

"No, it isn't. You may be going to do something in the future. Who knows? The Defense Department doesn't generally arrest people before they decide to commit a terrorist act."

"That's not me. Never has been. Never will be."

Sam shrugged. "If you say so."

"I do!"

"All right, tell me about yourself."

Ben's eyes widened. "Now?"

"We've got time."

"I thought fighter jets were on their way?"

"They are," Sam admitted. "But what are you going to do? Get out and push? It's not like we can make the JetRanger go any faster than it's already traveling."

"All right," Ben drawled, "I'm a half-human scion of some kind of alien race or something..."

"They're not an alien race, just ancient," Sam corrected. "And I meant what really happened to you? What's the deal about Bolshoi Zayatsky?"

"I have no idea. I'd never even heard of the place before today. I have no idea where it is even."

Sam blinked and said, "Russia."

"That's right!" Ben yelled, as though he'd just remembered. "He said it was in Russia!"

"Who did?"

"Special Agent Ryan Devereaux."

"Who's he?"

"I have no idea. The man who interrogated me. He said my parents were from a terrorist organization in Russia. That's all I know."

Sam turned and met his eye. "Were they?"

"Beats me," Ben announced. "I mean, I don't think so. They both died in a horrible car accident when I was three."

"What did they do before they died?"

"They traveled a lot."

"Really?" Sam raised his eyebrow. "To Russia?"

"No. Never. Only ever in the USA. They were substitute teachers," Ben said, as though that justified things.

"Okay, what do you know?"

"I'm the son of two perfectly normal people, John and Jenny Gellie. I don't know how far back my family goes in America; I've never really cared. But I know that all four of my grandparents lived here, in the States, until their deaths. My family didn't sneak over here or anything like that."

"And your parents?"

"Like I said, my parents died when I was three years old, which was after the death of most of my grandparents. Grandma Gellie was still alive, but she wasn't in the best of health — there was no way she could have coped with a three-year-old boy on her own. So I was fostered by my parents' best friends, the Fulchers. I don't remember much about my own parents. I remember my father reading me bedtime stories with him balanced on the edge of my bed. I remember my mother chasing me through the house for hide and seek. I remember what they actually looked like better from photographs than from their real faces in my memory, but what do you expect? I was three."

Sam remained silent but gave a curt nod, like he was listening.

Ben took it as encouragement and continued. "The Fulchers made pretty good replacement parents, even though they'd never intended to be parents in the first place. They loved me and supported me, and gave me good advice. If it wasn't for them, I probably never would have made it past my anger at my parents' death. It hung around for a long time. I'd lost everything I'd ever known, and the only people I had to blame were them. I'm sure I broke their hearts about a million times, until I grew up enough to understand how much I was hurting them."

"And you said you now work at the State Department?"

"That's right," Ben nodded. "I'm a junior law graduate."

"Good for you." Sam smiled kindly. "I mean, for someone in your position, a background in law has gotta help, right?"

"You'd think so. But according to Special Agent Devereaux, all those rights go out the window when you're suspected of terrorism. Obviously those rights disappear when you donate blood too."

"What happened at the hospital?"

"I went to the hospital in order to donate blood because my friend was in a motorcycle accident, and the hospital's blood supplies were getting low. I volunteered to show up and donate. I've never donated before, but it was more because I didn't get my ass in gear than for any real reason. I've always meant to, I just never got around to it — until today."

Sam made a wry smile. "Guess you're not going to become a regular?"

"No. Never again. I mean, I wanted to help, but not if this is the outcome."

"So tell me what happened when they took your blood?"

"I didn't know what the actual procedure for donating blood was supposed to be. They started taking multiple samples for tests. You'd think they'd be able to just take the blood donation and test it for whatever they needed to test it for...after the donor had left the building. Now that I've had two minutes to think about it, it seems especially odd, what they did. Tests. More tests. Still more tests!"

"How many blood samples did they need?"

"At least seven before I eventually got fed up and tried to leave. But they stopped me. They tried to talk me out of it, they tried to get in my way, and finally they injected me with something that knocked me unconscious."

Sam's eyes narrowed, questioningly. "After that, you woke up in the interrogation room of the Pentagon?"

"That's right. I woke up tied to a chair with tuff-ties, which I can't imagine would be considered even remotely professional unless you were at a riot or something, I don't know, where a bunch of prisoners had to be restrained for a relatively short period of time. Then Devereaux appeared and started questioning me. Just one of them at first. Asking me all kinds of intrusive questions. Why are my eyes violet? Have I ever been sick? What was my real age? Who were my parents, really?"

"Yeah, I'm seeing it."

"I feel like they got the wrong guy, like I have a look-alike who's sitting in a waiting room somewhere, waiting to get interrogated, and getting bored because everyone has forgotten all about him."

"Maybe this is all a mix up," Sam said. They looked pretty serious though... maybe something about your parents makes you special? Maybe you're genetically different than everyone else?"

"I don't want to be special. I don't want to have a secret background. You know what? I have a pretty good life. I don't have a secret fantasy about being someone else, some kind of weird-ass chosen one or something like that," Ben said, defiantly. "My parents are my parents. My life is my life. I'm not some kind of sleeper terrorist, like that agent was trying to imply. I don't want to wake up one morning and be Arnold Schwarzenegger in Total Recall. I'm happy the way I am, and I don't need this crap."

Sam tried to take all that in. He tried to read between the lines for some kind of gap between Ben's words and the man who was sitting beside him in the JetRanger.

"You did pretty good taking me hostage for a guy with no military experience."

Ben shrugged. "Football in high school and college. Running back. I was pretty good, too. Could have made it big, but I had other plans."

"You were holding back. You're agile enough that you could have gone pro, if that's what you wanted."

"Maybe I didn't feel like taking football too seriously. It's just a game. Besides, it's one of those jobs. You get injured you're out."

"Did you? Get injured?"

"No. Never."

"Do you do any drugs? For football or otherwise?"

"I tried weed in high school. Just to be friendly. But no steroids or experimental drugs or anything hard. I never had any need for them."

Sam shook his head, his lips curled into a slight grin.

"What?" Ben asked.

"I don't know. I'm just trying to work out if you're the most unlucky son of a bitch, or the best liar I've ever met."

In the distance three Earth shattering explosions filled the velvet of night. They were followed by the loudest clap of thunder Sam had ever heard. They seemed to shatter the entire sky.

Ben squinted, his eyes searching the clear horizon for the sound's origin. "What was that?"

"Sonic booms," Sam replied.

"From what?"

"My guess…F16 Fighting Falcons!"

Ben felt his gut lurch with the inherent rise in fear of something sinister approaching. "What does that mean?"

Sam swallowed hard. "They've found us."

CHAPTER FIFTEEN

S AM BANKED THE helicopter to the right, taking a northern course into the Appalachian Mountains and the densely forested Shenandoah National Park. He dipped the nose, descending hard into an unknown valley.

Fifty feet off the valley floor, he pulled the cyclic collective back, leveling the JetRanger until it was riding just above the canopy of the thick forest below.

Ben shouted, "You have any idea where we're going?"

"Not a clue," Sam replied, taking the helicopter so close to the spur of the mountain that he had to watch that its rotor blades didn't nick the tree line. "But we have to find somewhere to put down before those fighter jets reach us."

"Agreed." Ben played with the JetRanger's GPS digital map. "It says we're over the Shenandoah National Park."

"It sounds like a beautiful spot, but that doesn't help me much!"

"What do you need?" Ben asked.

"I need a clearing!" Sam replied, his voice only just able to be heard over the whir of the rotor blades overhead. "Somewhere we can put down, where the fighter jets can't follow us."

"They won't be able to spot us once we're on the ground. I've hiked in the Shenandoah National Park. The forest canopy is so dense it's hard to see out and impossible for an aircraft spotter to see in."

"That's great, but I still need that clearing!"

Ben said, "I'm looking! I'm looking!"

High above them, three F16s raced by, the flames of their afterburners leaving a trail like rockets in the sky above.

Sam said, "I suggest you look faster!"

"I found it!" Ben yelled.

"Where?"

"Over the next ridge at your nine o'clock!"

Sam's eyes darted toward the ridge. "That's the peak of a mountain!"

Ben ignored the semantics. "On the other side is a deep valley, in which the Piney River runs. There's a small clearing a couple of klicks north of it."

"That's the best you can do?" Sam asked, turning his head to look across his shoulder, where the fighter jets had headed. "It won't take those fighter pilots long to realize we've turned off I-211!"

Ben looked at him through raised eyebrows. "You got a better idea?"

Sam gritted his teeth. He didn't. "All right. Here goes."

He banked to the left, following the natural curvature of the mountain range, keeping his nose mere feet off the tree lined ridge. In the darkness of night, the canopy looked like a blanket of black velvet, impenetrable to his gaze.

Behind him he heard the sound of the fighter jets changing direction.

As soon as the JetRanger cleared the crest of the mountain range, he lowered the nose and raced down into the deep valley below. With no moonlight penetrating the valley to assist his vision, the river below appeared a slightly darker shade of black.

Sam brought the helicopter down toward the river, careful not to let the rotor blades overhead catch on the valley wall.

Three F16 Fighting Falcons raced through the valley, coming within twenty feet of the JetRanger before racing by, pulling up hard, and racing toward the sky in a near vertical display of the jets' raw power, then disappearing over the distant ridgeline.

Sam glanced at his radio, confirming that it was still set to the local frequency. None of the fighter jet pilots had tried to communicate with him. He expected they would have tried to direct him to a specific landing location of their choice, but instead they had flown by without a delivering a single radio transmission.

It was impossible to think that they had missed him completely. The squadron of F16s flew close enough that Sam could see the whites of the pilot's eyes as they raced past.

Ben asked, "What the hell are they doing?"

"I don't know. A reconnaissance flyover, I guess."

"Now what?"

"I don't know," Sam replied. "Maybe they send in a helicopter with a team of elite soldiers on board just to make sure they don't lose you. I don't know, but I'm not sure if it's still in our interest to land."

"Can you turn around, find somewhere else to land?"

Sam nodded. "We can try that."

He slowed the helicopter to a near stop and planted his foot on the left pedal, turning the JetRanger round on its axis until they were facing the way they had come.

Sam lifted the nose of the helicopter and raced along the steep slope of the valley wall. They needed to get out of the valley if they were to lose the F16s before they returned for a second flyover. The forest was a dense mixture of chestnut, oak, spruce, fir, and poplar tulips.

He wondered how much of a radar shadow they would provide.

Above them, he spotted the three F16s flying in formation. They were making a broad turn, setting up to fly above the valley, in a bombing run.

Sam swallowed hard. "Get your harness unhooked."

Ben looked blank. "What?"

A flash erupted from the wing of the first fighter jet, followed immediately by a second one.

"Jump."

"Are you fucking crazy?"

Sam peeled out of his harness and ripped the helmet's comm cord out of the panel. He threw the JetRanger door open. No time to waste arguing with a civilian.

It might already be too late.

"Jump!" he shouted, already putting action to word.

CHAPTER SIXTEEN

THE VIP VH-60 Black Hawks of the Army's 12th Aviation Battalion's Executive Flight Detachment raced across the Shenandoah Valley.

In the executive seats at the rear Tom Bower sat next to the Secretary of Defense. He took in a long, slow breath.

The Secretary of Defense was on her cell phone, speaking to the commander of the F16 squadron out at Joint Airforce Base Andrews, telling him that the F16s were to locate and maintain a visual of the JetRanger and nothing more.

Her voice was raised above the whir of the Black Hawk's rotor blades.

Three simultaneous blasts lit up the velvety black sky.

Tom's heart raced with disbelief. He didn't need to look out the helicopter's window. He'd flown helicopters in Afghanistan in 2003. He knew that sound well. It was an AIM-120 AMRAAM—Advanced Medium Range Air to Air Missile—being fired.

Nor did he have to check and see if they hit their target.

The AIM-120 AMRAAM was a high-supersonic, all weather, Beyond Visual Range, fire-and-forget air-to-air missile. It used a high-explosive warhead and relied entirely on active radar homing for the final stages of flight, meaning if the pilot pulled the trigger, it was going to reach its intended target.

That target, in this case, was a JetRanger with Sam Reilly on board.

No chance it would miss and impossible to believe that anyone would survive when it did.

In a dark and deadly-sounding voice, the Secretary said, "What the unholy fuck were they thinking? I ordered them not to fire!"

Nobody in the helicopter dared respond.

Tom licked his lips. The helicopter flew closer to the wreckage site. A ball of smoke still hung in the air. More rose from the ground where the helicopter had crashed.

Tom chewed on his lip as the helicopter circled around a second time.

"Take it down," the Secretary said.

"Where?"

"Anywhere you can."

"Yes, ma'am."

The pilot circled the wreckage, before heading off to the north in search of a landing site.

Tom shook his head. He was going to have to break the news to Sam's parents. His eyes turned to the Secretary. If her look was any indication, heads were going to roll.

CHAPTER SEVENTEEN

SHENANDOAH NATIONAL PARK

S AM RECOGNIZED THE white-top of the converted VH-60 Black Hawks of the Army's 12th Aviation Battalion's Executive Flight Detachment as it circled above the crash site nearly two hundred feet away. He tried to take a deep breath, but his chest hurt where multiple thick branches had clashed and almost certainly fractured his ribs on his way down. It was the dense foliage of the forest that had reduced the speed of his fall to somewhere within the vicinity of survivability. He exhaled slowly, gritted his teeth, and shuffled his back up against the trunk of a large poplar tree.

The blaze from the downed helicopter sent a soft glow radiating across the fuselage of the VIP helicopter. Sam's eyes were swimming, but he could make out the vibrant sky blue of the DoD seal on the side of the bird.

Was the Secretary of Defense on board?

His eyes narrowed.

Did she order the F16 pilots to shoot him down?

He shook his head. There would be time to find out what happened and why, but right now he needed to conserve his strength and energy in order to escape.

Sam's eyes tracked the VIP helicopter as it flew overhead

without stopping and continued farther along and into the valley. He expelled a deep breath of air. It was impossible for anyone above to spot him through the forest's dense canopy. He shook his head. Someone had tried to kill Ben Gellie. That wasn't a warning shot. Those pilots were ordered to hunt Ben down and take him out. There was no attempt to get him to land the helicopter and surrender. No negotiations. Just cold-blooded murder. His bloodied lips curled upward into a determined grin as the realization struck him every bit as hard as the branches — someone had tried to kill him.

They knew that he was on board the JetRanger. His own people knew that he'd been taken hostage and that he was piloting the helicopter. They were flying over Shenandoah National Park, away from any populated region, which meant there was no risk of direct terrorist threat. No reason why the F16 Fighting Falcon pilots couldn't attempt to force them to land. But there weren't any communications...

They had just tried to kill him!

Sam tried to blink away the blur of disorientation.

Why had someone from the Pentagon ordered his death?

The skies were now empty of any aircraft, leaving him to the silence of the forest. Scattered among the chirping crickets was a distinct glow up ahead where the crackling of fire from the downed helicopter was threatening to start a wildfire.

If the blaze took hold, it could engulf the forest and race up the valley faster than he or Ben could possibly outrun. They needed to get moving — quickly.

His eyes raked the ground, searching for any signs of his captor, turning skyward before settling on a dense section of foliage in the canopy high above to the south where something moved. It could have been an owl or a squirrel. He couldn't be sure.

"Ben?" he said, more remembering the fact of his existence than trying to find the guy.

There was no reply.

Sam stood up, grimacing as blood rushed through his aching legs. It hurt but he could bear weight and all his limbs responded to his instructions. He might still have damage to his internal organs and for all he knew, he was bleeding to death internally, but at least his spine was intact.

The fire crackled in the distance.

It was starting to take hold on the nearby poplar trees. Whatever injuries Sam had could wait. If they didn't get out of there soon, those injuries would be the least of his problems.

He cupped his hands and shouted, "Ben! Are you alive?"

"Up here!" Ben's voice came back.

Sam stared at him through squinted eyes, his brow furrowed. Ben was stuck approximately 25 feet in the air on the upper branches of a birch tree.

"You okay?"

"Fine," Ben replied with a rueful grin. "First they lock me up for donating blood and tell me I'm America's terrorist suspect number one. Then, when I escape and take you hostage, they shoot us down without so much as a warning shot! At your suggestion, I just jumped out of a moving helicopter, fifty feet off the ground!"

Sam grinned. "You're welcome."

Ben wasn't finished yet. "Now, the fall that was supposed to kill me, leaves me stranded up here to take another gamble with my life. So how do you think I feel?"

Sam ignored the question. "Can you move?"

"I'm twenty-five feet off the ground. What do you think?"

"The fire at the crash site is starting to ignite the forest," Sam said. "It's struggling to take hold this early in the spring, but it won't be long—and when it does, we'll have no chance to outrun it. So, I think you're going to have to work out a way to get down!"

Ben's gaze snapped round toward the rising conflagration. He cursed. "All right, all right! I'm going to try to see if I can reach that branch over there."

Sam ran his eyes across the lower branches of the birch tree. There weren't many. It looked like the lower half of the tree had been intentionally stripped of its branches years ago, either by bears or National Parks Rangers in an attempt to clear the canopy and make way for some of the other nearby trees to grow.

Either way, it looked like there was a lot of empty air between Ben and the ground.

"What branch?" Sam asked.

Ben didn't reply.

Instead, he bent his legs, gritted his teeth, and set his eyes on the fork of a nearby poplar tree. It looked like seven or eight feet. A distance difficult to make with a run up, but almost certainly impossible from standstill.

You've got to be kidding me!

"You sure you want to go for that one?" Sam asked.

"No," Ben replied. Then, glancing at the blaze from the nearby wreckage of the helicopter, he said, "It looks like I'm going to have to anyway."

"What if you try…"

Sam stopped midsentence.

Ben launched himself toward the poplar tree. His right hand connected on the fork of the tree where a straggling offshoot took his weight for a split second, before snapping.

Ben swore and a moment later he was free falling toward the ground — landing on top of a pair of juvenile conifer trees.

Sam raced over to meet him. "Are you all right?"

"Yeah, fine. We should be dead," Ben complained, as he opened his eyes, patted himself down, confirming that he was mostly uninjured, and stood up. "They just shot us out of the sky!"

"Hey, you don't look hurt," Sam pointed out. "Let's get going."

Ben glanced at the thick forest. "Where?"

"West. It won't take more than a couple days for the investigation team to reach here. Then it won't take long, a day or two at best, before they realize the wreckage is distinctly missing any bodies."

"And when that happens, they're going to double up on their search effort," replied Ben.

"Which means, we have two days to get as far away from here as possible."

Behind them, the blaze of the wrecked helicopter finally overcame the nearby trees, which now started to crackle as the flames engulfed them on its eager attempt to race to the crest of the nearby mountain.

Sam yelled, "Run!"

CHAPTER EIGHTEEN

B EN'S HEAD SNAPPED round, his eyes darting toward the ominous glow that threatened to engulf them. The thick forest was in the process of becoming a cinder box, burning out of control. Ideally, they needed to get below the fire, but already it was spreading laterally along the steep slope. It was too late; they needed to reach the crest before the fire overwhelmed them.

Sam was already off running up hill at full speed.

Ben didn't need any further encouragement. He climbed the steep hill at a pace that would have made his old football coach proud.

The helicopter had been shot down more than two thirds of the way to the top of the ridgeline. The dense Shenandoah Forest thinned toward the crest, making it easier to scramble their way through, rather than fighting their way through the dense undergrowth of the lower sections of the mountain.

Behind him the inferno raged.

Its fire burned greedily through the highly flammable foliage of the conifer trees, ripping through the new rosebuds of the poplar trees, and dancing between the undergrowth of the chestnut trees. The heated air raced upward, sending a torrent of fiery wind their way.

Ben breathed the hot air through his throbbing lungs, the muscles of his legs burned and his chest pounded.

He caught up with Sam and quickly outpaced him.

The ridgeline was now within sight, less than a hundred feet above them. The gradient increased to seventy-five and then eighty degrees and he found himself clinging to the straggling trees for support as he dug the balls of his feet deep into the soft soil and climbed.

In the dark, the final twenty feet to the summit looked like an ominous wall of darkness, an impossible silhouette to overcome. He couldn't see how they were going to summit the last twenty or so feet, which appeared to be more like an open rockface, but it didn't matter. The fire was lapping at their toes and would overcome them any minute. There was no option of turning back now; they would just have to find a way to reach the top.

A shallow stream ran from the nearby peak forming the base of a small waterfall with the runoff of the last of the melting snow from winter. The misting water now bombarded the wildfire, clashing with it head on, instantly turning to steam with a sibilant hiss.

The ground above him became difficult to visualize.

Blood pounded in the back of his head and Death teased at his heels, but still Ben ran onward, placing one hand in front of the other as he scrambled up the near vertical slope.

His hand reached the vertical granite outcrop.

He tried to grip it and climb, but the misting waterfall made the stone wet and slippery. No matter which way he positioned his hands, he couldn't quite get enough perch to climb.

Ben swore. "We're trapped!"

"Keep moving to your right!" Sam replied. "There's a cave!"

Ben couldn't see it, but he kept moving anyway. It wasn't like he had another choice. He was wedged between an unassailable vertical cliff and a raging fire.

Keeping his left hand on the rocky wall, he kept moving to the right, until he disappeared into a fissure in the rock.

The flame lit up the entire rockface like a spotlight, leaving an

CHRISTOPHER CARTWRIGHT | 103

empty void where the rock opened into a deep crevasse.

His eyes frantically searched his surroundings for another way out, but came up short. They were now trapped.

Sam shouted, "Into the cave!"

"I don't think I can fit..."

"You don't have a choice!"

Ben squeezed into the narrow fissure, feeling with his hands and feet as he shuffled deeper. With his head turned to the side, he maneuvered his body blindly inside.

"Quick!" Sam shouted, following him in.

Ben felt the searing heat of the fire front run to greet them. He held his breath, as though that might protect his lungs, closed his eyes, and took another step deeper.

But his feet didn't find their footings.

Instead, they found nothing but an empty void.

Ben screamed...

As he slipped, free falling, deep into the rocky abyss.

CHAPTER NINETEEN

OFFICE OF THE CHAIRMAN OF THE JOINT CHIEFS OF STAFF— PENTAGON

T HE SECRETARY OF Defense stormed along the hallway toward the office of the Chairman of the Joint Chiefs of Staff.

A junior aide tried to stop her. "I'm sorry, Madam Secretary, General Painter is in a meeting."

"Let me see him—now!" Her words were barked out with the authority of her position.

"I'm sorry, ma'am…"

She ignored the military aide and opened the door. "Who the hell authorized your F16s to shoot down a helicopter carrying Sam Reilly?"

The President stood up. "That would be me."

She felt deflated. "For God's sake, why, Mr. President?"

"We have DNA confirmation that Ben's parents were John and Jenny Gellie."

The Secretary of Defense pursed her lips, feeling the crushing weight of what she now realized was about to come next. "And?"

"The very same ones who were involved in the Bolshoi Zayatsky incident…"

She paused, remaining silent.

"Did you hear what I said, Madam Secretary?"

"Yes, Mr. President."

His blue eyes smiled triumphantly. "Madam Secretary?"

"Are you certain it's him?"

"We have his DNA. It's a match." The President raised an eyebrow slightly. "Now what do you say?"

The Secretary expelled a deep breath. "Thank God you killed them before he got away."

"I'm glad we're in agreement."

She said, "I want people there now to retrieve the body."

"They're on their way, but..." his eyes turned downward.

"What?"

"The crash caused a forest fire. I'm afraid the entire place is ablaze. We might need to wait a day or two until the fire passes before our team can reach the helicopter."

"Just make sure someone's there the second that fire stops burning... I want DNA proof the bastard's dead!"

CHAPTER TWENTY

SHENANDOAH MOUNTAIN

S AM REACHED FOR Ben's outstretched hand.
Their fingers locked on each other's forearms. A gust of wind blew a series of red hot embers into the rocky fissure. Sam swore as a few sparks embedded onto his back. He shifted his footing to dip down and brace for the incoming barrage of heat. His left foot slipped. It wasn't much, but it was enough to unbalance him.

Ben tightened his grip and a moment later, Sam slipped into the deep chasm of the void below.

The rocky crevasse angled eighty-five degrees downward. It was formed by two giant stone walls placed at an angle, some two feet apart, and less than a dozen feet wide to form a massive slide. Sam frantically swung his arms outward trying to find something to perch his hands and grip to arrest his fall. His fingertips connected to the smooth wall of stone, slipping freely.

Sam bent his knees and tried pushing upward to form a wedge between the two rocky structures. He was dealing in seconds and microseconds to stop his descent, before speed and momentum would make it impossible.

Those seconds passed and Sam kept sliding.

His speed raced toward a lethal velocity.

Sam bent his knees slightly and angled his toes outward,

ready to absorb the violent end to his downward progression.

Seconds went by.

For every one of them, he knew his speed was becoming closer to terminal.

By the fourth second the ground on his back disappeared completely and for another millisecond he was free-falling into a great expanse of a pitch-black void.

His toes were the first to strike the icy cold water, followed immediately by his entire body and head. Sam heard the whoosh of water rushing over his body, followed by the emphatic thumping of his heart in the back of his ears.

Sam's feet hit the rocky bottom without warning.

His bent knees took the worst of the jarring impact and a moment later he straightened them again, pushing up from the rocky riverbed.

He kicked hard and prayed he was swimming in the right direction. In the darkness it was hard to orient himself to the water's surface. His lungs started to burn and his legs stung with exertion as lactic acid built up.

An instant later his head broke the icy surface of the alpine, subterranean river.

He took in a deep gulp of fresh air.

The icy water stung him all over. But at least he could still move everything, which meant that he couldn't be that badly injured. It was the cold that would get to them. They would freeze to death if they didn't find a way out soon and get dry and warm.

That thought reminded him of his unwanted companion.

"Ben?"

No response.

The place was eerily silent.

A hidden river, an ancient passage of icy water through the subterranean depths of an alpine mountain. No light and almost no movement.

Was this to be his final resting tomb?

"Ben Gellie!" Sam shouted.

The words echoed, revealing the chasm was much larger than he'd first expected.

Still no response.

He gently swam to the edge of the cavern. There was no bank. Only a vertical stone wall. Sam turned, and mentally tried to begin drawing a map of his surroundings. The only light he could muster was the backlight of his dive watch, which did little in the way of allowing him to visualize his new surroundings.

The dive watch showed that he was still at an elevation of 3,723 feet. He recollected from his younger days hiking the Appalachian Trail that most areas of the Shenandoah Valley were roughly 3,000 feet above sea level. That meant that despite falling some distance from the mountain's original peak of 4,397 feet, they were still high up in the mountain range.

He continued swimming across the water until he reached the edge of the river. This section also led to a vertical wall of stone, impossible for him to climb. Sam marked the location in the mental diagram that he'd formed, and turned ninety degrees. It took him a couple minutes to the next wall. This time, it was less of a vertical wall and more of a narrowing tunnel, where the roof seemed to progressively shrink to the height of the river, before disappearing completely.

He swallowed as he imagined this could possibly lead to the only way out.

There was a chance that he might be able to hold his breath and dive through it, but there was no certainty that it didn't lead to a submerged body of water that lasted hundreds of feet. In the dark, it would be impossible to make such a dive.

Sam marked the location and turned to commence his swim to the opposite end of the subterranean cavern.

"Ben!" Sam shouted. "You alive?"

Again, no response.

The only sound in the cave was the gentle lapping of water as he swam across the stilled river.

This was the longest swim he'd had to do so far.

The longer it lasted the more his gut twisted with fear and hope — that deadly combination. If it went far enough, he might be able to swim his way out of there to freedom. If not, he was just swimming farther away from all hope.

Already, his body no longer felt cold.

That wasn't a good sign. It meant he was entering the early stages of hypothermia. If he wasn't going in the right direction, there was a good chance he wouldn't have enough energy to turn around and make it back again.

Up ahead he heard the sound of water splashing.

"Sam!" came Ben's voice in the dark. "Are you still there?"

"I'm here! Are you all right?"

"Yeah, I'm good," came Ben's cheerful reply. "But you've got to get over here quick; you're never going to believe what I've found!"

CHAPTER TWENTY-ONE

S AM KICKED HIS legs, swimming toward Ben's voice.
He opened his eyes and spotted a faint light coming from a narrow choke point up ahead. Two broken rock pieces leaned on each other to form a natural arch no more than a foot above the waterline, through which a pale glow was radiating, at the edge of which was the distinct outline of Ben's face.

For a split-second Sam thought he could just make out Ben's grin.

"What did you find?" he asked. "An opening?"

"No," Ben replied. "But I think we've found a guide to show us the way."

Sam was too tired to ask any more questions. "Show me!"

Ben nodded. "Through here."

Ben ducked under the narrow rock arch, dipping his head underwater and disappearing below. Sam took a couple deep breaths and followed after.

The slender opening was no more than a foot wide and Sam had to swim through with his hands held far ahead until they gripped the edge of the rock wall, allowing him to pull the rest of his body through.

On the other side of the choke point he found his arms able to reach freely into an open body of water. He kicked his legs and swam toward the surface.

Surfacing in the new cavern, Sam wiped his face to clear the moisture from his eyes. The new grotto was somehow larger than the previous one, only narrower and much longer. A blue haze shined down and reflected on the crystal-clear water. Sam's gaze traced its way along the vertical granite walls toward the cathedral vault high above—settling on more than a thousand stars.

Only they weren't stars.

They were moving with purpose and at a speed much too fast.

Their scientific name was Lampyridae, a family of insects in the beetle order Coleoptera. They were winged beetles, commonly called fireflies or lightning bugs for their conspicuous use of bioluminescence during twilight to attract mates or prey. The little beetles produced a cold light, with no infrared or ultraviolet frequencies, by using chemicals to produce light from the lower abdomen often yellow, green, or pale red, with wavelengths from 510 to 670 nanometers. Sam recalled from his early science classes that the Eastern US was home to the species *Phausis reticulata,* which emits a steady blue light.

Massed in the thousands, this group of beetles formed the image of an artificial river of blue in the cathedral vault high above, steadily flowing outward—to their freedom.

Sam said, "Follow them!"

"Sounds good," Ben replied, starting to stroke arm over arm across the surface of the water, following their flying guides on their way out of the grotto. "I'm freezing!"

The width of the vaulted cavern alternated as they progressed through the subterranean river, sometimes getting bigger and other times getting smaller.

In the darkness of the first cavern it was impossible to tell whether or not the water was flowing, but with the radiant blue light of the fireflies, Sam noticed for the first time there was a small drift in the same direction as the glowing creatures.

He smiled at his good fortune.

They were all going the same way.

Sam continued swimming for several minutes before having to pause for a beat to regather his strength. The icy cold water was stripping him of his stamina. Stretching out on his back to increase buoyancy and conserve his energy, he realized the flow of the river started to noticeably pick up its speed.

The cavern was coming to another choke point up ahead and all the water was being squeezed through a narrow gap. He ran his eyes across the swarm of fireflies. They were branching out at the narrow section and bulging like a torrent of flood water churning and overflowing an obstacle in its path. Their wings whipped together to create a high pitched whir that resonated throughout the cavern like a diesel engine under strain. It was a deafening sound that seemed almost impossible to have originated from any number of beetles.

Sam dropped his gaze until it reached the empty void between the surface of the water and the swelling banks of the artificial, glowing blue river of bioluminescence. There was a new color mixed in together, too. It was a deep orange, the sort of color one would see reflected from a full moon through dense smoke. Wind howled through this section.

His pulse quickened.

With it, so did the speed of the river.

They were about to reach the opening to the outside world. The question was, where did the water come out?

Twenty feet ahead of him, Ben tried to turn around and swim backward. Something had frightened him. But there was nothing Ben could do about it. The man was now fully trapped in the powerful current. The walls of the crevasse were slippery and the tug of the flowing water too powerful. Despite Ben's best effort, he continued to progress toward the pinch point at the opening.

And a moment later, he was sucked through and

disappeared.

Sam felt the uneasy rise of fear in his throat.

He toyed with the idea of trying his luck at out-swimming the current, but dismissed the idea immediately. He was a strong swimmer, but it was unlikely he'd be able to beat it, and besides, where else would he go? Sam knew he had to get out of the water soon or hypothermia would kill him as surely as any disaster that could be waiting for him on the other side.

Sam relaxed and drifted, letting the current take him to greet whatever had startled Ben Gellie so much. There was a sort of peace that comes with a decision that is a certainty. There were no other options left for him, which meant that he needed to work with the decision to travel through the opening, and deal with whatever might be waiting for him.

The current dropped him down a shallow cataract before whipping him toward the opening.

Sam held his breath and opened his eyes.

An instant later, he felt his heart lurch with impending doom. He gritted his teeth and readied himself for death, because in that moment, he realized that he was wrong about the fireflies making the roaring sound. He had been wrong all along. Even a thousand flying beetles wouldn't make that sort of sound. As soon as he spotted it, he knew where the vibrating sound originated—a giant waterfall!

Sam felt the water beneath him disappear.

He was free falling, more than a hundred feet off the ground.

Game over…

There was nothing he could do to save himself!

CHAPTER TWENTY-TWO

T IME MOVED SLOWLY.

They say it does when you see your own death race toward you. Like some type of primal part of the brain recognizes a threat that can't be beaten and therefore decides to plaster the dying images, frame-by-frame, across the visual cortex.

Adrenaline, noradrenaline, and cortisol rushed through his body at infinitesimal speeds and Sam Reilly's internal video recorder started to feed him each image of his impending death, in that frame-by-frame manner.

He was no longer frightened. No reason to be. There was nothing more he could do about it. He'd played every last card he'd been dealt and lost.

But there was something someone else could do about it.

The recorder inside his brain stopped running.

A firm hand gripped his wrist hard. His descent stopped with a jarring force in his right shoulder that threatened to rip his arm from its socket. The motion swung him toward the side of the mountain, beneath the waterfall.

His wet shoes were the first to hit the rock wall with a thud.

Sam's lips curled with incredulity as his eyes leveled at Ben Gellie, who was hanging precariously by one arm from the branch of an oak tree that appeared to be holding onto the edge of the mountain with even less likelihood.

Ben pulled his arm backward and Sam reached the rock face of the mountain.

"Thank you," Sam said, "for saving my life."

"You're welcome. Without you I would have never jumped from the helicopter and I'd still be sitting inside its charred remains."

Sam shrugged. "Forget about it. The question now is, where do we go from here?"

Ben pointed to a dilapidated iron chain, bolted into the side of the mountain a few feet above them, leading to the entrance of the subterranean river. "Over there! It looks like someone's previously tried to explore that waterway."

Sam ran his gaze over the rocky climb to the chain. It was difficult, but not impossible. His wet shoes would make things more dangerous, but it could be done. Everything seemed possible now that he'd survived what should have been his certain death.

"Okay," he nodded. His vision turned to the valley below. "The question is, where is here?"

"The Shenandoah Valley," Ben replied without hesitation.

Sam studied the valley in the gray light of predawn.

Surrounded by ancient mountains, the Shenandoah River cut a gentle and incredibly flat valley into the landscape. From memory, he recalled that part of the valley was a National Park, and the pastoral scenes are framed by a lush deciduous forest growing on the hills.

"All right, that's something," Sam said. "At least we know where we are. Let's try and reach that chain. If we don't get warm soon, hypothermia will properly set in and we'll die."

"Agreed."

Ben scrambled up the short crack in the rock to reach the permanent chain above. Despite the cold, he moved with the agility of a seasoned rock climber.

Sam gritted his teeth, focused on each individual hold, trying to forget he was still a couple hundred feet off the ground, and scrambled to the chain. His left hand reached it first, followed an instant later by his right—both hands locking with the strength of fear.

Ben didn't wait to discuss their next plan. Instead, he followed the chain as it led across the rockface, before finally ending at a narrow ledge approximately two feet wide. It wasn't much, but Sam noticed it was enough for someone like Ben, who appeared to have no fear of heights, to walk freely.

Sam on the other hand, who had a pathological fear of heights, knew it would cause trouble. Such an experience would ordinarily render him to a crawl, but he was driven to walk across the ledge—driven by the thrill of a second chance at life and a need to get warm.

The ledge terminated at a steam track leading along the mountain in a gentle decline, before reaching the lush deciduous forest at the base of the hills.

Sam and Ben continued in silence.

At the tree line, Ben stopped and faced Sam. "We should light a fire and get warm."

"Agreed," Sam replied. "I saw a log house down along the river. We should head there."

"It might be occupied."

Sam shrugged. "Even better. They might already have a fire going."

Ben's eyes narrowed. "They might tell someone about two strangers who wandered out of the woods…"

"It's a risk we're going to have to take."

"Are you sure that's a good idea?"

Sam said, "Do you have a lighter?"

"No."

"Then, I'm sure. We'll freeze to death before long if we don't start a fire and get warm and dry."

"All right. Let's go check out the log house."

Twenty minutes later and after a brisk walk, Sam and Ben reached the bank of the Shenandoah River, upon which a large wooden building had been constructed. The place was a vacation camp, servicing adventurous youth.

A wire fence ran around the entire place and the gate at the front was secured with a heavy steel chain and padlock.

"It appears we've arrived too early in the season for the camp to be open," Sam said, picking up a small river stone.

"It would appear so," Ben agreed. His eyes drifted toward the stone Sam was carrying and Ben's lips curled into a wry grin. "What are you hoping to achieve with that?"

"We need to break the lock. Unless you want to wait around until summer camp starts?"

"You won't have a hope in hell of doing so with that. A padlock like that will take any amount of hammering you're prepared to give it with that stone."

Sam leveled his eyes on Ben. "You got a better idea?"

Ben removed two small metal picks from his wallet. "We could just open the lock."

"You're kidding."

Ben ignored his skepticism, silently inserting the twin picks in the keyhole of the padlock and working them with the delicate and fastidious movements of an expert locksmith or a thief. It took him exactly twenty-two seconds to unlock it.

"Ta dah! What do you think of that?"

Sam looked him directly in the eye and said, "I'd like to know how a lawyer with the State Department became so proficient at breaking and entering."

Ben grinned. "Technically, it's just entering. The lock will still work once we leave."

CHAPTER TWENTY-THREE

T HE CAMPFIRE WAS burning within ten minutes.
Sam cupped his hands, warming them by the delectable radiant heat. Having borrowed some blankets from the camp supplies, he and Ben stripped from their wet clothes and placed them by the fire to dry.

He stared out the window.

Red and blue lights flickered across the moonlit water of the large river from the opposite bank of the river to the one that the summer camp was based. It was the second wave of fire trucks and emergency workers preparing to defend the small township that resided within the Shenandoah Valley.

Sam asked, "Any idea the name of that river?"

Ben nodded. "It's called the Shenandoah and it runs a farther fifty-six miles south of here before reaching the Potomac at Harpers Ferry."

"Could you be any more specific?"

Ben pointed palms skyward. "Hey, you asked, I give the answers."

"Really?" Sam met his eye. "How could you be that certain?"

Ben removed his cell phone from a zipped pocket. "Because I checked a few minutes ago."

Sam blurted out, "You still have your cell phone!"

Ben shrugged. "Yeah, why? Did you think I threw it out after we crashed? It's coming in quite handy, you know."

Sam snatched the cell phone out of Ben's hands and threw it into the fire.

Ben grabbed the stoker and tried to retrieve his cell, but within seconds the fire had already done its irrevocable damage. "Hey! What the hell did you do that for?"

"We're supposed to be dead! Killed in a helicopter crash nearly five miles from here…"

"Yeah, so?"

Sam sighed heavily. Perhaps intelligence wasn't a genetic trait passed on to Ben. "So, don't you think it might seem strange that a dead guy's phone kept walking after being killed?"

Ben avoided Sam's penetrating gaze, as his flashed with fear and shame. "What difference does it make to you?"

"I don't want to get caught any more than you do."

Ben asked, "You're staying with me?"

"I sure am."

"Why?" Ben met his eye with incredulity. "I don't have the gun anymore. I lost it when I jumped free from the JetRanger. You're free to go. I have no way to keep you prisoner anymore, so why stay?"

Sam set his jaw. "Because someone picked a fight with the wrong person."

"They sure did," Ben said, his voice filled with gravel and defiance. "But it's not your fight."

"Yeah, it is." Sam grinned. "They made that abundantly clear when they tried to kill me in the process!"

Ben asked, "You're really going to stay and help me?"

"Sure. Why not?"

"We might get killed."

Sam shrugged. "Whatever's going on here, I think it's safe to say someone will always be trying to kill us unless we get to the bottom of this, and fix it once and for all."

"That's the real question. How do we fix it?" Ben said, "I mean, we can keep running, but at some stage if we want to finish it, we need to find out what's really going on and why."

"Agreed. You're right. We can't just keep running forever. First thing we need to do once we're out of here is work out who or what they think you are. Once we do that, we might just find out who exactly wants you dead, and why."

"And how that person is connected to the long reach of the Department of Defense."

Sam rubbed his thawing hands together in front of the fire. "So far, we know this has something to do with what your parents did—or someone thinks they did—back in Bolshoi Zayatsky. We know that you were born lucky, with the good fortune to rarely if ever, get sick, and never seriously unwell. You look young for your age and have naturally fast reflexes that would have put you in line to play sports at a professional level. Anything I missed?"

"Yeah, I have purple eyes."

"Right. Purple eyes. As you pointed out, so did Elizabeth Taylor and a couple thousand other people throughout history, but it is an extremely rare genetic anomaly—and Special Agent Devereaux certainly seemed to have honed into that detail. It's not a lot to go off."

"Barely anything at all."

Sam said, "We can search for terrorist events or any unique event for that matter in Bolshoi Zayatsky, particularly around the mid to late seventies. It's a stretch, but even a simple Google search might point us in the right direction if there was a terrorist organization there at the time."

Ben's lips flattened into a hard line. "There wasn't."

"You're sure?"

"Hundred percent."

"How?"

"I already had a look."

"But the first you'd heard of Bolshoi Zayatsky was when you were being interrogated at the Pentagon."

"I checked on my smartphone — before you threw it in the fire."

"Right." Sam nodded, a slight grin forming on his lips. "What about your parents. Do you know where they were buried? It might sound a little ghoulish, but the only definitive way to determine the truth about your genetic lineage might be to exhume their bodies and crossmatch their DNA with yours."

"I'm afraid that's not possible."

"Too ghoulish?"

"No. Just not possible. Both my parents were cremated."

"Where are their ashes now?"

"Scattered across the Yosemite Valley."

Sam nodded. "All right, that might make it a little difficult," Sam agreed. "What about a picture?"

"Yes, just one. I've kept it with me all these years, but I don't see what you can do with it." Ben handed him the photo from his wallet. "Here have a look at it."

Sam took the photograph, a Polaroid, and examined the image.

It showed two adults in a cave — presumably his real parents — and a small child standing inside with them. Sam studied their faces. His father was roughly the same age as Ben was today, and could have easily passed as his brother. There was no doubt in Sam's mind that the man was his real father.

Sam met Ben's eye. "This is your family?"

Ben nodded. "As far as I know. I don't recall their faces. You know, I look at this picture, and I feel like it was real. I even recognize the location, but I can't in all honesty say I recognize my parents. Does that sound crazy?"

Sam tilted his head, trying not to look at him directly. "You were very young. It's easy to forget."

"That's just it. I don't forget. I have what the doctors tell me is an eidetic memory—an ability to vividly recall images from memory after only a few instances of exposure, with a high precision for a brief time after exposure, without using a mnemonic device—and yet, I can't remember my own parents. Does that sound strange to you?"

"Like I said, you were very young. Even the best of memories can't be expected to hold true at that age."

Ben's eyes welled up. "I've stared at this photo more times than I'd like to admit, searching it for some sort of clue about where I came from. I've always known I was different. Always have. Sometimes I don't even look at the photo, I just search the image I have indelibly embedded in my mind."

"And still you find nothing?"

"Not a thing."

"But you remember the location?"

"No. I remember exploring the location. It was surreal, like something out of one's fantasy... I've often thought if I could just find the cave, it would jog my memory, and maybe reveal something about my past that it appears my parents have gone to great lengths to withhold from me."

Sam smiled. The story was sounding more and more like just that, the imagination of a child, longing to recall the past, rather than to recall anywhere in particular. "I have a friend who's pretty good with computers. When we get out of here, and we get a new cell phone, I'll send her a copy of the photo and see what she can find. Maybe she can correlate the image with a cave on her database."

Sam's eyes turned to the cave itself. It had a unique purple hue to it. A crepuscular beam shined down on the polished rockface behind them, making it stand out like a prized painting at a gallery.

Something about the image caught his eye.

There were elaborate pictograms etched into the rockface. The photo's resolution wasn't good enough to make out the intricate details, but there was no doubt about the basic design. He stared at the drawings etched into the rockface for a minute.

There were seven in total.

Each one depicted a human face. Although, the more Sam looked at them, the more he doubted whether that was true, deciding that they were most decidedly near-human. A missing link on the scale of evolution, perhaps? He would need the expert advice of an anthropologist, but at a guess, he thought the faces were of cavemen.

Sam handed the photo back to Ben without saying anything.

Ben took it, his jaw set and his eyes fixed with defiance. "Well? Go on. Aren't you going to ask the question?"

Sam grinned. "What question?"

"The same one everyone asks. The first thing everyone wonders when they look at the photo."

Sam grinned. "Okay, what's the story with the ancient faces?"

Ben nodded. "Every person who's ever seen that photo has asked the same question."

"What's the answer?" Sam challenged him.

"I have no idea who the strange masks belong to. I've spent years searching for some reference of them, but have found nothing. I've looked for the cave, too, without any luck."

Sam nodded. "I wouldn't expect anyone to have had any."

"Why?"

"Because, if my instinct is right, that cave has been buried in perpetuity and the identity of those faces long forgotten."

Ben patted his hanging pants to see if they were dry yet. "So then what do we do?"

Sam replied without hesitation. "We head to North Dakota."

"Really?" Ben asked. "What's in North Dakota?"

"Someone who might just be able to give us answers about why you're so valuable… or dangerous to the world."

"All right, sounds good. You got a plan how we're going to get there?"

"I've got some ideas, but it depends."

"On what?"

"How you feel about white water rafting the Shenandoah River during the spring runoff?"

CHAPTER TWENTY-FOUR

I T WAS 8 A.M. before Sam woke up.

He'd had just three hours sleep in the past twenty-four hours. There was no way of knowing how long that wildfire would burn. Already, there was a good chance the wreckage of the helicopter might be accessible. And when it was, they would discover no bodies. He could just imagine the subsequent manhunt that would unfold.

No. Three hours would have to do. He and Ben needed to get moving.

They picked the first raft they found in the summer camp's storage lockers. The thing was mildly deflated after spending the winter out of the water in storage. Ben found a pump and it didn't take long to have it fully inflated again.

Sam broke into the emergency supplies locker and found some out-of-date canned food — vegetable stew — bottled water, blankets, first aid kit, and a map of the whitewater rapids.

By 8:30 a.m. the six-person whitewater raft was loaded with supplies and paddles. Sam and Ben donned a pair of wetsuits, helmets and lifejackets. They placed their now dry clothes into a dry bag, and pulled the raft onto the bank of the Shenandoah River.

"You sure you want to do this?" Ben asked.

Sam ran his eyes across the wide river. It was flowing, but didn't look all that dangerous in the daylight. He nodded.

"Yeah, this looks like the fastest way to cover ground. Why not?"

"Well, for one thing, it's spring. That means the winter snow has melted and its runoff is feeding this river, making it flow much faster and meaner. Didn't you think it was strange no one else is on the river yet?"

"Hadn't really thought of it."

Ben's face crunched up into a slight grimace. "Only the die-hard rafters would even attempt the river this time of the year."

"The die-hard rafters and those running for their lives." Sam grinned. "Come on; let's get this raft in the water."

"All right. Can't say I didn't warn you though."

Sam stepped barefoot into the shallow water at the edge of the river. The water felt like liquid ice as it stung at his protesting lower legs. He dragged the raft deeper.

When the water reached the top of his knee, Ben climbed into the back of the inflatable and he said, "Come on, Sam. Get out of that cold water!"

Sam pushed down hard on the bow of the inflatable raft, taking his weight off the ground and swung his legs over the edge and into the boat. He picked up a paddle, and together, in silence, the two men synchronized their paddling until they were into the deeper, faster flowing river, where the powerful current caught them.

The raft drifted downriver over the course of the next hour without any concerns, comfortably following the natural course of the river, before reaching the first set of dangerous rapids. Normally only shallow ripples, the spring runoff meant that the section was now rated more like a class III or IV set of rapids.

Sam's eyes darted between the upcoming rapids and Ben. "What do you think?"

Ben sighed. "I don't think we have a choice. Let's just ride it out."

Sam shrugged. "All right, let's do it."

The raft dipped over the first cataract, dropping nearly eight feet in a swift movement. Sam shifted his weight to the back, as the bow punched through the naturally forming recirculating and trapping current known as a hydraulic.

White water washed into the boat.

Sam and Ben hit their paddles hard, trying to gain enough forward momentum to break the current's hold on them.

Up ahead they narrowly missed a large boulder, before dropping off the side of the next cataract. This time, the current caught the large raft, immediately sending it sideways.

The inflatable started to lift on the left side.

"High side!" Sam shouted, as he threw his weight down on the lifting section of the boat.

"I'm on it!" Ben replied.

Ben reacted fast, shifting his body weight so that he was almost entirely out of the raft. The boat started to turn in a strange spiral motion, until the stern caught the main current and the raft shot out of the hydraulic.

They drifted down another set of shallow drops, fighting the current and washing machine effect of the turbid waters for another twenty minutes before the river settled into a more docile calm.

Sam caught his breath and assessed the boat. It had held up well without any puncture or damage. Their cargo, stored in water tight containers, and secured to the raft by rope, were all over the place—some not even inside anymore.

He pulled them inside.

Ben glanced at him. "Thanks. We don't have much, but it's nice to keep what we do have."

"Agreed."

Sam settled into the raft, stretching out, as the river calmed. He studied the deciduous forest that lined the Shenandoah River. There was chestnut oak, red oak, and tulip poplar, intermingled with spruce-fir. A diverse array of wildflowers blossomed throughout the shallow scrubs and green grasses.

As they drifted farther downriver, Sam gazed upon the seemingly countless ferns and scrub species found beneath the trees. There were multicolored azaleas and lady slipper orchids. Purple-pink Eastern Redbud blooms and bright green buds filled the landscape set upon the backdrop of mountain ranges.

A pair of baby black bears foraged on blueberries on the river's bank, while their mother kept a guarded watch. Her eyes met Sam's with casual indifference. It obviously wasn't the first time she'd spotted a raft drifting lazily down the river.

A military helicopter passed overhead. Sam watched it for a minute, before it banked to the east and continued onward. The pilot was clearly searching for something — most likely them.

Ben asked, "What if they start to search the river?"

"Then we hide the raft, and find somewhere to lie low until they pass. They'll be searching in a series of grids. Once they finish their fly overs they'll move on to the next zone." Sam ran his eyes across the dense bank of the river as it met the narrowing rocky valley; they were quickly losing hiding places. "Isn't there some massive limestone cavern somewhere here? Maybe we can hide out in there for a while."

"Yeah, a town called Grottoes. Home of the Grand Cavern, America's oldest show cave, open to visitors since 1806. I visited it once as a kid. The cave was used by the Confederate and Union soldiers to hide during the Civil War."

Sam nodded. "That sounds good. We can use that if we need to lay low for a while."

"No, we can't."

"Why not?"

Ben shook his head emphatically. "It's about fifty miles south of here, upriver."

"All right, then we'll just have to make sure we're gone by the time they start their search of the river."

His eyes swept the Shenandoah Valley. Surrounded by

ancient mountains, the Shenandoah River cut a gentle and incredibly flat valley into the landscape. Its lush pastoral scenes were framed by a vibrant deciduous forest growing on the hills.

Sam's mind wandered to its history. However peaceful it may now appear, the history of the Shenandoah Valley Civil War tells of a time when sacrifice was the currency that bought freedom. Riddled with old battlefields and Civil War cemeteries, the valley had earned the peace and harmony of the present day.

The rocky valley narrowed as the next set of rapids emerged.

A quick glance at the map they'd taken from the summer camp, showed them aptly named, Bull's Tail, the Shenandoah's mile-long Staircase, Mad Dog, White Horse, Hesitation Ledge, and Roller Coaster.

The raft rode these at speed.

With the higher water levels of the spring runoff, the rapids at this section were less harsh than earlier along the river. The massive torrent worked to speed up their progress rather than hinder it for once.

At the bottom of the final set of rapids, Sam spotted a series of blue herons, ospreys, and bald eagles feasting on the abundant trout, discombobulated by their navigation of the rapids.

As the water slowed, Sam and Ben continued to paddle downstream until the river widened into the confluence of the Shenandoah and Potomac rivers at the tripoint of Virginia, West Virginia, and Maryland.

They passed the Harpers Ferry National Historical Park and a sign that noted that this was the view Thomas Jefferson claimed was "worth a trip across the Atlantic."

The raft drifted farther along and a few paddle strokes set them alongside a jetty. Sam and Ben opened their dry bags, trading their wetsuits, life jackets, and helmets for their clothes and shoes.

Ben glanced at the raft, its presence conspicuous as the first one for the season. "What do you want to do with this?"

Sam spoke without hesitation. "Push it back into the river. Maybe we'll get lucky and someone will find it at Knoxville or even farther along the Potomac and assume we got off there."

CHAPTER TWENTY-FIVE

HARPERS FERRY

B EN OPENED HIS wallet. "I have thirty-five dollars in cash, what do you have?"

Sam opened his wallet, licked his lips and frowned. "I have a fifty."

"That's it?" Ben looked at him through slightly narrowed eyes. "I thought you were the rich son of a shipping mogul?"

"Sure, but this is the new century. No one carries cash anymore."

"Great. So, we have eighty-five dollars to get from here to North Dakota. Maybe we should skip the railway and just start hitch-hiking from here?"

"Nah, that's all right," Sam said, holding his hand out. "Hand me what you've got. Eighty-five will probably do for what we want, anyway."

"Really?"

"Sure. Hand over the cash."

Ben handed him the cash, his jaw set firm, the lines deepening beneath his eyes.

Sam took the cash, without bothering to put any of it into his wallet. "Thanks. I'll be back in a second."

"Where are you going?"

"That general store over there."

Ben asked, "What are you going to buy?"

"A cell phone."

"Really?" Ben's eyes flashed. "We have eighty-five dollars to get us from here to North Dakota and you want to spend it on a cell phone?"

Sam smiled. "Yeah, why not?"

Ben sighed. "All right. You want me to come?"

"No. That will only make it more likely someone will recognize us later when the FBI starts to show our faces everywhere. You can wait here. Actually, better yet, head over to the train station, and find out what it costs to take a train to the next stop."

"Which direction?"

Sam said, "I don't care. Whichever way the next train's heading."

"Okay."

Sam walked into the general store and returned a couple minutes later as the proud owner of a brand-new Nokia 3110C cellular phone—an updated version of the original popular Nokia from a decade earlier, and a tribute to those who just wanted a cell phone to make calls.

Ben returned. "I hope you didn't spend all our money. There's a train leaving for Martinsburg in half an hour. It costs nine dollars-fifty for a single ticket."

"Great. That'll do."

Ben's eyes lowered. As he ran them across the strange device in Sam's hand, his face crunched up as though he was examining an alien device. "What is that?"

Sam lifted it up proudly. "This is what forty-eight dollars and fifty cents gets you these days in cellular technology."

"What do you do with it?" Ben asked. "There's no LCD

screen. How do you access the internet?"

"You don't."

"Then what did you buy it for?"

"To make a phone call."

"Really?" Ben was incredulous. "We're down to thirty-six dollars fifty, because you want to make a phone call!"

Sam shrugged. "It's an important call."

"Who are you going to ring?"

"A good friend of mine. She's good with computers. I have an idea she can help us out of this mess…"

Ben warned, "They might be tracking her calls."

"Not this one."

"Are you sure? They are the government; they can authorize anything they want. If this thing's as big as you think it is, they won't let a little thing like the Fourth Amendment get in the way of things."

Sam shook his head. "Doesn't matter if they do or don't. No one can hack my friend's system."

"He's that good, is he?"

"No. He's a she. And she's even better than that."

Ben's reply was immediate and emphatic, "Every phone can be hacked."

"Not this one."

"All right. If you say so."

Sam said, "I do say so. Now pass me the photo of your family. I need to send her a copy."

Ben handed it to him.

Sam stared at the old cell phone. It had an integrated 1.3-megapixel camera with up to 8x digital zoom that was considered extraordinary back in its heyday in early 2007. He placed the 2.5 x 3.5-inch photo that Ben had given him onto a park table and tried to take a picture.

The phone made an audible click sound as it snapped the picture.

He stared at the screen trying to make out the image. The 1.8-inch display supported a maximum resolution of 128 × 160. It captured a basic outline of the image, but Sam doubted Elise could do much with its resolution.

Ben looked over his shoulder. "You think she can see that?"

"Probably not, but it's worth a try. Hey, stand still for a moment."

Ben looked at him. Sam took another picture. This time it was of Ben's face.

"Hey, what was that for?"

"Sentimental value."

"Right."

Sam dialed a phone number by heart.

"Yes?" a soft, female voice answered.

"Elise, it's Sam! I'm alive but I need help."

"What's new?" Elise replied, teasingly. "I hadn't heard you were meant to be dead. Weren't you heading off on a vacation while the *Maria Helena's* replacement was being built at the Quonset Shipyard?"

"I was." Sam glanced at Ben and smiled. "Something held me up."

"Oh Sam, when will you learn to take a break?" she chided.

"I'm working on it but I need your help."

"Sure, what do you need?"

"We're about to catch a train to Martinsburg. I need you to order something to be delivered from there to North Dakota. Something big. Something that will fit in a shipping container if you know what I mean. Also, you might want to add some food and clothes for us."

"Sam. Of all the places you want to go right now, you've chosen to visit her?"

Sam stared vacantly at a pair of mallards diving for fish upon the glistening surface of the Potomac River, his mind much further away, recalling fond times long since passed. He shook his head. "It's not about her. I need answers and right now she might just be the only person who can provide them."

"All right. I'll organize a shipment delivered to Martinsburg to be loaded on the next freight train bound for North Dakota." Sam heard the staccato of fingers on keys, typing in the background. "The next freight train leaves at 3 a.m. I'll text you with details soon."

"Thanks. Now, I need you to find everything you can find on a man named Ben Gellie. I'll text you an image of his face and his last known address."

"Okay, anything else?"

"Yeah. There's a photo of Ben with his parents taken in the seventies. I need you to locate the cave for me."

"Have you tried Googling the image?"

"Yeah. Elise, we've tried the usual paths. Now we need your expertise."

"Okay. What about his parents. You want to know where they are now?"

"That would be great. Their names were John and Jenny Gellie. They have a record with the CIA, but I have no idea what it says. The FBI says they're terrorists. Something they did a long time ago."

"Do you have a last known address?"

"I'll text it to you, but I'm not sure it will do you any good."

"How come?"

"They moved in 1978."

"Any idea where?"

"No. They faked their deaths in '78."

"I'll see what I can do."

"Thanks, Elise."

"Sam." There was a slight hesitation in her voice.

"Yes?"

"This man, Ben Gellie, is he dangerous?"

"I don't know," Sam said, looking him right in the eye. "But right now, the FBI believes he's the most dangerous person in the world."

CHAPTER TWENTY-SIX

PENTAGON, VIRGINIA

T HE SECRETARY OF Defense picked up the phone.
Without preamble she said, "Tell me you've got his body."

"I'm afraid not, ma'am," replied Devereaux.

"And what about Sam Reilly?"

"His body's missing too."

"Really?" The secretary took a deep breath. "All right. They have a forty-hour head start. With no money and nowhere to go, they can't have gotten too far."

"Agreed."

"And Devereaux…"

"Yes?"

"This time make certain he's dead for Christ's sake!"

"Yes ma'am."

CHAPTER TWENTY-SEVEN

PENTAGON, VIRGINIA

TOM BOWER ENTERED the private office at the Pentagon.
He had been picked up at the motel he'd slept at last night—although slept being the operative word, he did very little of it—while he awaited news direct from the helicopter wreck site, and was escorted by Special Agent Ryan Devereaux back to the Pentagon. On the way, Devereaux had said very little. His tone, curt and dispassionate, made it clear that it wasn't going to be a friendly meeting. Tom figured the guy's team at the FBI was in trouble. After all, it was their stuff up that made them lose a suspected terrorist and eventually get his best friend, Sam Reilly, killed. Maybe they were looking for a scapegoat.

Well, that wasn't going to be him. He and Sam's only involvement was that they were leaving the Secretary of Defense's office at the time the man was trying to escape. It wasn't like any of them could have chosen to do anything different.

The hostage taker was the one with the Glock.

Tom ran his eyes across the room.

There was a single desk and a recliner chair with a set of thick Tuff-ties broken on the ground. The place was clearly an interrogation room—presumably the same one from which the fugitive, Ben Gellie, had escaped.

It was clearly meant to be an intimidation tactic. Tom bridled. Who did these guys think he was? It would take more than an unkempt interrogation room in the Pentagon to put him on edge. His father had been an admiral in the U.S. Navy, he'd spent six years flying helicopters in the marines, and seen active service in Afghanistan, Iraq, and Istanbul. Not to mention for the past decade he'd worked for Sam Reilly, which had exposed him to some of the greatest risks of his life.

Special Agent Devereaux threw a thick manila folder on the desk.

Tom opened it, taking it in at a glance. The file had no name, but a service number, rank, and proficiency marks. It might have looked like a school report card. This one was used for induction training in the military.

Tom leveled his contempt-filled gaze at Devereaux. "And this is?"

"Sam Reilly's induction training records."

"So?"

"What do you think?"

"I think my friend has a relatively high IQ, above average stamina, an inhuman fear of heights and enclosed spaces, and he can shoot better than ninety-nine out of every hundred soldiers out there."

"That score makes him a better marksman than every nine-hundred and ninety-nine soldiers out of a thousand, who took the test." Devereaux shook his head as though it was a personal afront. "In fact, in the year he completed his induction training he achieved the highest overall scores of any person on the course — not just his course — but any SEAL course that year."

Tom shrugged. "So? I told you the guy was smart, tenacious, and patriotic."

"Sure," Devereaux said, leveling his dark brown eyes at him, with his palms held outward in a conciliatory gesture. "So now you see where we're coming from?"

Tom crossed his arms. "Afraid not. You'd better explain it to me, because right now, all you're doing is confirming what we already knew — America lost one of its greatest patriots."

Devereaux stared at him through narrowed eyes. "You haven't heard?"

"Heard what?"

"Our team reached the crash site early today — there were no bodies in the wreckage."

Tom felt his heart thump. "Sam's still alive?"

"It would appear so." Devereaux sighed heavily. "And with him is Ben Gellie. So, now you must see my problem with Mr. Reilly."

Tom was still focusing on the newfound knowledge that his friend was alive. "I'm afraid I still don't get where you're headed."

"Well," Devereaux said, picking up the manila folder. "What I see here is a man who graduated from the marines with the highest ability for hand to hand combat and weapons combat. He's out there with my suspect, who we believe has no formal military training."

"Again. So what?"

"So, don't you think it's a little hard to swallow that someone with no military training could keep someone with Sam Reilly's background hostage, while they race through the wilderness?"

Tom expelled a deep breath. "You think he's working with the terrorist?"

"I do, son."

Tom shook his head. "You're nuts."

"The report doesn't lie."

"Yeah. Well, you know what else the report says here… Sam Reilly is one of the most disciplined, loyal, and trustworthy people on Earth. He would never betray his own country."

Devereaux shook his head. "You really believe that, don't

144 | THE HOLY GRAIL

you?"

Tom stood up. "I'm finished here. I suggest you get back to doing your job and try and locate your suspect and my friend."

"Mr. Bower," Devereaux said, his voice hard and menacing. "If you receive any word from Sam Reilly, be sure to contact me straight away. Anything you withhold from here on in could be considered treason, and given the stakes, I don't think the FBI would look favorably on your chances of ever seeing the outside of a federal prison again."

"Are you threatening me?"

"Not at all, Mr. Bower. I just wanted to be certain that I make myself clear."

Tom opened the door. "Go do your job. I can see myself out."

Devereaux shrugged. "Suit yourself."

Tom reached the end of wedge three at the Pentagon, walked out the main doors, and into the visitor's carpark. There he climbed into his rental car — a Toyota Camry — started the engine and drove off along Rotary Road.

A blue taxi came to an abrupt stop in front of him.

Tom had to jam on the brakes.

A woman with short brown hair got out. She wasn't tall, but neither was she particularly short. She turned and walked toward him with a distinctive purpose in her stride.

She opened the passenger side door and got in.

Tom beamed with pleasure. "Hello Genevieve! You're one hell of a nice sight to see!"

CHAPTER TWENTY-EIGHT

"**D**RIVE," SHE ORDERED without preamble.

Tom shifted his foot over to the accelerator. "Where to?"

"Take the next exit onto the Jefferson Davis highway. We have a flight to catch at Ronald Reagan National Airport."

Tom smiled, happy to see his girl again and wishing that he had more time to embrace her. "Where are we headed?"

"Arkhangelsk Oblast, Russia."

Tom grinned. "Obviously."

He drove on, waiting for more of an explanation, but getting nothing but silence.

"All right," he said, "I'll bite. I hear the weather's pretty cold in Arkhangelsk Oblast this time of year, so do you mind telling me what's in Oblast?"

"The Bolshoi Zayatsky Island."

Tom turned off the highway and into the airport. He pulled into the first parking bay, lifted the handbrake, and switched off the car. He turned and kissed her firmly on the lips, letting his lips linger there as long as he could, before she broke the embrace.

"Why are we going to Bolshoi Zayatsky Island, Genevieve?"

"Elise just contacted me. Sam's alive. He needs our help."

"He's in Russia?"

"No. We don't know where he is. It's safer that way. Safer for everyone."

Tom understood the principle of a stopgap in spy networks, but how this related to he and Sam, he couldn't even guess. Still, he trusted the man with his life and was willing to give him a bit of room to work with. "What does he need?"

"He wants us to check out a lead. Something about his captor's past, the reason the FBI thought he was a Russian terrorist, everything leads back to Bolshoi Zayatsky Island."

Tom asked, "What's on the island?"

"A two and a half thousand-year-old series of stone labyrinths."

"Really?" Tom's lips curled into a wry smile. "Did you mention that neither of us usually work archeological sites? Maybe we should contact Billy?"

Dr. Billy Swan was an expert archeologist and anthropologist, who had worked closely with Sam Reilly and his team on a number of occasions, specifically focusing on the ancient race known as the Master Builders.

She was also Tom's ex-girlfriend.

Genevieve shook her head. "According to Elise, the ancient texts were written in Russian, so unless Billy took a recent crash course in the language, I'm the best bet to translate the texts written on the ancient ruins. Besides, she's off the grid currently."

Tom withheld a smile. "Elise already tried?"

Genevieve tilted her head, her lips parting in a coy smile that was entirely fake. "Yes, she already tried. We're Sam's second-best chance at working this out."

"Okay."

Genevieve went to open the door.

Tom reached over and stopped her. Leaning in close to Genevieve's ear, he asked, "What does any of this have to do with Sam and his captor?"

Genevieve whispered, "Ben Gellie's parents were allegedly leaders of a Russian terrorist organization. They followed an ancient Russian text that predicted an exact date and time for the ending of the present-day order of the world. There were multiple interpretations, but most pointed to a widespread plague that would decimate the Earth's population of *Homo sapiens,* allowing another species to rise up from the ashes. The ancient site even referred to a virus, named the Phoenix Plague. By the looks of things, Ben's parents attempted to make the prediction come true."

"When was this supposed to take place?"

"Before the end of this year."

"So what happened to Ben's parents?"

"The CIA got lucky. Someone from within the cult's team betrayed them. A black ops team was sanctioned to end their program back in 1975."

"What went wrong?" Tom asked.

Genevieve said, "They destroyed the cult, but its two ringleaders—John and Jenny Gellie—somehow escaped."

CHAPTER TWENTY-NINE

SHENANDOAH NATIONAL PARK

THE BOEING AH-64 Apache helicopter was built to be a predator.

It was an American built, twin-turboshaft attack helicopter with a tailwheel-type landing gear arrangement and a tandem cockpit for a crew of two, with the pilot sitting behind and above the co-pilot-come-gunner.

Powered by two General Electric T700 turboshaft engines with high-mounted exhausts on either side of the fuselage, the machine looked like an unearthly beast, designed for nothing but death. At its nose were sensors mounted for target acquisition and night vision systems. It was armed with a 1.18-inch M230 chain gun carried between the main landing gear, under the aircraft's forward fuselage, and four hardpoints mounted on stub-wing pylons carried a combination of AGM-114 Hellfire missiles and Hydra 70 rocket pods.

It was a bird of prey, designed to search and destroy.

The Apache flew along the Shenandoah River, circled the summer camp at the bend of the river, and landed on the soft mud at the bank. Its quad-bladed main rotor and tail rotor — designed to increase survivability during attack — continued to turn at speed.

Special Agent Ryan Devereaux opened the door of the

Apache, climbed down the three ladder rungs, and stepped onto the ground. He ducked his head out of instinct, despite the height of the rotor blades being far above him.

He greeted the manager of the summer camp who had reported the intrusion. They spoke for a few minutes and then he climbed back on board the Apache helicopter.

Once inside, the pilot asked, "What did he say?"

Devereaux grinned. "They were here up until twenty-four hours ago. They stole a raft and presumably put it into the Shenandoah."

"How far can they get?"

"According to the manager at the camp, they could make it all the way to the Potomac and then all the way to Chesapeake Bay."

"Great. You want me to run the distance of the river?" the pilot asked.

"Yeah, until someone else gets me better intel!"

The two General Electric T700 turboshaft engines screamed as their RPM reached take-off speed. An instant later, the attack helicopter was in the air.

Its pilot flew fast and low above the Shenandoah River.

Twenty miles downriver Devereaux said, "New plan, we're heading to Leesburg."

"Understood, sir," the pilot replied, taking the Apache up to a higher altitude. "What do you know?"

"A kayaker at Leesburg just reported finding the summer camp's raft along the shore."

"He's certain it's ours?"

Devereaux smiled. "Yeah. He's certain. The raft has the summer camp's name printed all over it. The man even gave us the boat number, which we've matched to the one stolen. So, yeah, that's our raft!"

The pilot flew above the Shenandoah Valley, cutting across

the land in a due east bearing at Bluemont. The helicopter circled the bend in the river where the raft had washed up on the shore. The banks were lined with Red Maple and River Birch, opening to clearings with verdant fields and bucolic homesteads.

Devereaux swore.

Even if Ben had gotten off the raft here, it was going to be a nightmare to locate him.

The blue lights of local law enforcement flashed below. An officer signaled to them with waving arms.

Devereaux ordered, "Take us down."

"Yes, sir."

The bird landed in a field some thirty yards off the officer's car.

Devereaux climbed out, spoke to the officer and raced back into the gunner's seat.

"Get us back into the air!" he said. "They found them!"

"Where?"

"Getting on a train at Harpers Ferry — heading west."

"When?"

"Twenty minutes ago!"

The Apache raced toward Martinsburg.

At Martinsburg, the predator circled the railway station. The train was just departing.

The pilot asked, "What would you like me to do, sir? Should I follow the train or put us down?"

Deveraux opened his mouth to speak, paused. His eyes darting between the station and the departing train. "If you were a fugitive, where would you go? Would you stay and hide or just keep going?"

The pilot's response was visceral. "If the entire US Defense Department was after me, I'd run like hell and pray to God no one found me!"

"Me too," Devereaux said. "All right, we'll follow the train, get ahead of it and put me down at the next station. I'll find a team of local law enforcement to help search that train. This time, I'm going to make damned certain they don't leave that train alive."

CHAPTER THIRTY

MARTINSBURG

S AM TOOK A step back, concealing himself in the shadow of a large chestnut tree, as he watched the Apache attack helicopter. It hovered directly above the railway station for several minutes before flying ahead following the train, which was headed toward Pittsburgh.

He watched until the predator disappeared beyond the horizon.

"What the hell do they think I've done?" Ben asked. "This isn't a typical fugitive hunt. They're hunting me with a machine made for annihilation! It's like they're judge, jury, and executioner all rolled into one."

"Beats me," Sam replied. "Elise, my computer friend says there's a CIA report of a covert operation in Bolshoi Zayatsky in the seventies. It refers to a number of terrorists being sanctioned, and that your parents disappeared before our teams reached the island."

"What were my parents doing on the island in the first place?"

"I have no idea," Sam replied. "Most of the report has been redacted. I've asked some other friends of mine to go to the island and see if they can fill in the gaps."

"They won't just leave us alone here. Local law enforcement will be out in droves trying to spot us. Our train doesn't leave until three a.m. That's nearly eight hours away."

Sam said, "Our accommodation should arrive any minute now."

"Accommodation?" Ben asked. "Did your friend book us a hotel room or something?"

"Yeah, you might say that. This one's on wheels and will be traveling all the way to North Dakota."

"Really?"

"Yeah, here it is now."

Ben turned, his eyes tracking an eighteen-wheeler Mac Truck. On the back of the truck was a standard forty-foot shipping container.

The truck pulled up and alongside the road. Sam watched as the driver released the pressure from the airbrakes with a large hiss.

"Now what?" Ben asked.

"Just wait."

It took less than ten minutes before the driver shut down the engine, climbed out of the cabin, and walked away in the direction of a local diner.

Sam smiled and said, "Shall we?"

"What?"

"Check into our hotel."

Ben said, "Your friend ordered us a shipping container?"

"Among other things, yeah."

"Won't they notice if you break into it?"

"No. We're not going to break into it. This one has an electronic keypad."

Ben met his eye. "So we're slumming it all the way to North Dakota."

Sam said, "Sure. If that's what you want to call it."

He sauntered toward the truck, moving with the casual indifference of a man who was just trying to kill time. His shoulders relaxed but not slouched. His eyes drifting aimlessly at the scenery like he had nowhere better to be.

At the back of the truck he climbed onboard.

There was a single electronic keypad on the right-hand side. Sam entered the number Elise had given him.

The electronic locks released immediately.

He opened the heavy door until it was ajar just enough for he and Ben to slip through. Sam stepped in first. Ben followed a second later, pulling the steel door shut behind him.

"I can't see a thing," Ben complained.

Sam said, "Hang on. There should be a light switch somewhere around here."

He fumbled with a switchboard on his left, and found the one that activated the light.

The entire shipping container lit up inside.

"Holy shit!" Ben said, as his eyes raked the inside of their new abode.

Sam grinned. Despite its exterior appearance, the inside had the layout of a Manhattan apartment with high end furniture and fixtures, complete with a painting of a beach. Sam flicked another switch and two digital windows revealed the outside world on either side of the shipping container. The device worked by projecting a digital image of the outside, making the steel wall appear to disappear.

Ben asked, "What is this place?"

"It's a self-contained one-bedroom apartment. A company in Baltimore produces and delivers them anywhere in the world — at a price."

"Elise must have worked magic to get it here so quickly."

"That magic you're referring to is most likely called cash and

I have no doubt she paid a lot of it. She also went to the trouble of having them pack some cold weather clothes for us, food, and hopefully a smartphone."

"Are we being trucked all the way?"

Sam opened the fridge and took out a bottle of soda and a ham and cheese subway sandwich. "No. This will be loaded on the freight train. Then it's about forty hours until we reach Minot in North Dakota."

Both men ate with the ravenous ferocity that the last forty-eight hours demanded.

When they were finished, Sam took off his boots, laid back onto the couch and reached a deep sleep within minutes.

CHAPTER THIRTY-ONE

BOLSHOI ZAYATSKY ISLAND, RUSSIA

THE RUSSIAN BUILT Ka-226T helicopter flew across the stilled waters of the White Sea and into Onega Bay. Its coaxial main rotor system and absent tail rotor produced a whisper quiet drone as it whirred by the coast, revealing their first glimpse at the Solovetsky Islands.

Genevieve banked the helicopter to the south, skirting the coast of the largest of the seven islands. Her eyes followed the coastal landscape, before fixing on a building. Built on the banks of Prosperity Bay, was the Solovetsky monastery, with its green and red tiled roofs and series of parapets. The fortified monastery was surrounded by massive walls with a height of thirty-three feet and a thickness of twelve. The walls incorporated seven gates and eight towers, made mainly of huge boulders up to fifteen feet in length. Inside, there were a series of religious buildings, all with interconnected roofs and arched passages.

She recalled that the monastery had been founded in 1436, but some said the place had been occupied by monks for centuries beforehand — having held a mysterious and ancient religious value that remained hidden to this day. It was one of the largest Christian citadels in northern Russia before it was converted into a Soviet prison and labor camp in 1926–39, and served as a prototype for the camps of the Gulag system.

It was the very place where her grandfather had risen to notoriety as one of the toughest prisoners, respected and feared by inmates and guards alike, eventually becoming dubbed the "Master of Slaves," before his release in 1953. His son, her father, having developed the same natural instinct for ruthless survival had gone on to set up one of the most feared and dangerous mafias within Russia. As an only child, Genevieve had grown up under her father's protection and instruction, where her mixture of beauty and deadly skills had eventually led her to a life as an enforcer for the mafia—a deadly assassin.

That was until ten years ago, when her father killed her lover and she'd decided to leave the family business—a sin within the family, punishable by death.

As a consequence, she took on a new name and persona, finding employment with Sam Reilly on board the Maria Helena.

Genevieve blinked, returning to the present.

Along the shore of the bay, a small amphibious seaplane was being tied up to a jetty. She recognized the aircraft as a Beriev Be-103 Bekas, constructed by the Komsomolsk-on-Amur Aircraft Production Association in Russia. It was designed for autonomous operation in the unmarked areas of Russia's far north and Siberia, the Be-103 was designed for short-haul routes in regions that have rivers, lakes and streams, but are otherwise inaccessible.

It had been years since she'd seen one.

A team of several men were loading some equipment from the seaplane onto an inflatable Zodiac. She wondered what they could possibly be delivering to the monastery.

She brought the helicopter back to straight and level, revealing her first glimpse of the Bolshoi Zayatsky Island.

Genevieve slowed the helicopter, before making a gentle bank to the right, circling round the island. It had been more than a decade since she'd flown the unique Ka-226T helicopter. It used twin main rotor blades which spun in opposing directions, allowing it to counteract torque and negate the need for a tail rotor blade.

It was a substantially forgiving aircraft.

Without a tail rotor the helicopter is safer on the ground and in the air, but it also makes it possible to use the Ka-226T in spaces with scant room for maneuver, as the fuselage does not extend beyond the area swept by the rotors.

Not that she would need that much room on the barren island.

She'd seen photos of the labyrinths but had never viewed them in person.

Her eyes swept the island, taking in some of the larger thirty-something labyrinths documented on its surface.

The labyrinths were constructed from local boulders set in rows on the ground in the form of spirals. Often there are two spirals set one into another, which has been likened to two serpents with their heads in the middle looking at each other. Intermittently along the spiral there are thicker or wider heaps of stones; the ends of the spirals are also wider. Each labyrinth has only one entrance, which also serves as the exit. The smallest labyrinth measures around eighteen feet in diameter, with the largest being seventy-five across.

"What do you think?" she asked.

Tom smiled. "Honestly, I don't know what I was expecting."

"You're not impressed?"

"They look like a lot of stones piled together to make spiral shapes."

"Hey, those spiral shapes have stood for two and a half thousand years."

"Don't get me wrong. That's impressive, I'm just saying I was expecting something bigger on the surface."

"Don't let the surface labyrinths fool you; the subterranean versions are much more impressive."

The island was part of the Solovetsky Islands, an archipelago of six separate islands, with Bolshoi Zayatsky being the second most southerly island in the group. It was a small island, having a total surface area of just 0.48 square miles.

The entrances to the labyrinths were all on the southern sides. The labyrinths have five types of settings, but each has only one entrance which also serves as an exit. Genevieve brought the helicopter to a hover, before landing on the southern end of the island.

She shut down the twin engines, turning her gaze toward Tom. "Seems bizarre that an ancient plan to develop a virus capable of ending the human race should have been developed on such a tiny, unimposing island."

"Everything about this seems unlikely," Tom agreed, the corners of his lips curling upward. "Are you sure Elise wasn't pulling your leg?"

"It's here…" Genevieve suppressed a grin. "Elise hacked into the FBI's records. The design for the Phoenix Plague was developed on this island more than two and a half thousand years ago, then a secret cult led by Ben Gellie's parents attempted to recreate the ancient virus."

"And what does Elise think we're going to find here?"

Genevieve shrugged. "I don't know. Answers."

"How? Surely the Black Ops team that infiltrated the cult would have destroyed everything."

"That's just it."

"What?"

"After the US Defense Department sanctioned the death of every member of the ancient Russian cult, it was determined to leave their prehistoric lab untouched, until they deciphered the meanings of the various pictographs."

Tom arched an eyebrow. "They left everything there for someone else to find and one day attempt to rebuild?"

She shook her head. "No. According to the Defense Department's archives, they were concerned that the completed Phoenix Plague had escaped and only the information stored within the ancient pictographs might reveal its antidote."

Tom opened the side door and stepped out. Genevieve followed him and slid the side storage compartment open. Above, the rotor blades slowed and whirred toward their eventual silence.

Tom asked, "Did they ever find it?"

"What?"

Tom said, "The antidote."

"No."

"But they left the ancient structure untouched?"

Genevieve nodded. "My guess is they're watching it remotely, just in case the ancient cult rears its ugly head again."

Tom leaned in and removed a pair of dive cylinders. "We'd better be quick then."

CHAPTER THIRTY-TWO

T OM AND GENEVIEVE slipped into their dry suits, donned their
SCUBA gear, and secured a pair of Heckler and Koch MP5
submachineguns onto the attachment of their buoyancy control
device. Each went through the systematic approach of checking
the other person's equipment.

All in total, it took less than ten minutes before they were
ready to hit the water.

Tom glanced at the closest labyrinth. It had been constructed
so that its entrance nearly touched the water's edge.

His eyes turned from it to Genevieve. "These labyrinths
aren't entirely unique to Bolshoi Zayatsky Island, are they?"

"No. I've heard similar designs are constructed throughout
northern Russia."

"All with the entrance facing the water's edge?"

Genevieve nodded. "I believe so. Why?"

"I read the various theories about their original purpose, and
when you remove all the mythical, religious, and superstitious
"gateway to the underworld" concepts, it really does leave you
with the most obvious hypothesis being that they were simply
elaborate fish traps."

"Yeah, I agree. I think so, too."

Tom smiled. "But there's one thing I really don't get."

She leveled her dark blue eyes at him, teasingly. "Just the

one?"

He ignored her jibe. "The greatest evidence that purports the idea that these labyrinths were used for fishing comes from the fact that all of the labyrinths in the region were built close to the sea and water levels were much higher two and a half thousand years ago, when it is believed they were constructed. The fish would have swum in through the entrance and become trapped in the labyrinth, making it easier for fishermen to retrieve their catch."

"I read the article. That seems to make sense to me. What don't you get?"

"If the water was higher when they built it, why then, is the labyrinth we're going to nearly a hundred feet below us?"

Genevieve grinned. "That's because the labyrinth we're going to was constructed a lot earlier."

"How much earlier?"

"About twenty thousand years to be exact."

CHAPTER THIRTY-THREE

TOM SWAM OUT a hundred feet, to where the water depth dropped dramatically. He dipped his head into the icy water. The White Sea was crisp with visibility extending all the way to the bottom some sixty feet away.

He glanced at the GPS reading on his dive computer.

They were right above the entrance. Back in 1975 a secret investigative team from the CIA tracked a group of suspected bioterrorists to the island, which was how the ancient labyrinth became known to the US Defense Department. That much made sense to Tom. What he didn't understand was how a group of civilians had located the ancient labyrinth in the first place — and more importantly, how they had managed to keep it a secret for so many years.

"You ready to dive?" he asked.

"Good to go," Genevieve replied.

Tom released some air from his buoyancy control device — BCD for short — and began his descent. After a few feet he started to swallow, allowing the air within his middle ear to equalize and avoid the pressure build up known as a "squeeze." There had been a time when he had to consciously do this every ten or so feet, but as the years went by and he started to count his dives in their thousands, the process came as naturally to him as breathing.

At thirty feet, he heard the high-pitched whine of a two-stroke motor.

His gaze drifted upward.

A rubber Zodiac raced by—toward the Bolshoi Zayatsky Island.

Genevieve caught the direction of his gaze. "They might be tourists."

Tom swallowed. "And they might not be."

"We've been in the water for less than ten minutes. No one knew where we were going. We didn't lodge any flight plans. It's impossible to think the CIA has had an elite team stationed here since 1975, just waiting for someone else to show up."

Tom continued his descent toward the entrance of the ancient labyrinth. "They might not be ours."

"You think someone else has been watching the island?" Genevieve asked. There was no fear in her voice, but plenty of intrigue and curiosity.

"I don't know."

Tom checked the bathymetric map on his dive pad, looking for the key identifying marks that would lead them to the labyrinth's entrance.

He kicked his fins, diving deeper as he followed the natural contour of the island's submerged shelf. At eighty feet he spotted what he was looking for.

Three large boulders. Each one roughly the height of an adult and shaped like an irregular sphere. They might have been naturally formed that way, or they may have been painstakingly chiseled and then rolled down into the water. Heck, if what Genevieve had told him was correct, and this ancient labyrinth was built somewhere in the vicinity of twenty thousand years ago, the White Sea would have been shallow enough that the entire entrance was out of the water.

Whatever the case may be, one of the stones definitely didn't belong there.

It was made of obsidian.

The rest of the stones were predominantly Jotnian sediments—a group of Precambrian rocks more specifically assigned to the Mesoproterozoic Era—predominantly a white quartz-rich sandstone or shale, with the silty seabed a mixture of mica and clay.

The result was a pitch black sphere on a bed of white stones.

Tom studied the out of place piece of obsidian. The entire surrounding geology of the White Sea was Jotnian sediments—and that meant no volcanic stone nearby.

Someone had gone to great efforts to shift the large piece of black volcanic rock to this location. Obsidian was used by a number of civilizations since the dawn of the Stone Age for a variety of purposes. The igneous rock was valued in Stone Age cultures because, like flint, it could be fractured to produce sharp blades or arrowheads. Like all glass and some other types of naturally occurring rocks, obsidian breaks with a characteristic conchoidal fracture. It was also polished to create early mirrors.

But the fact remained; only one group of people ever went to the effort of moving large amounts of obsidian stone for building purposes—the Master Builders.

Tom stared at the stone, as though it might reveal the correlation between Ben Gellie, the ancient Russian cult, and the Master Builders.

Modern archaeologists, he recalled, have developed a relative dating system called obsidian hydration dating, to calculate the age of obsidian artifacts.

He wondered what such a reading would say about the door—if that indeed was the dark sphere's purpose.

"Well?" Tom asked. "What do you think?"

"You want to know if we have the right place?"

"Yeah."

"There's only one way to find out."

Tom allowed some air into his BCD until he reached neutral

buoyancy. He stopped next to the dark sphere, placing his hands in a precise location, two thirds of the way toward the eastern edge.

He increased the pressure.

Nothing happened.

"What gives?" Tom asks.

"Try the opposite end of the door," Genevieve suggested.

Tom set up his hand positions, gently pushed inward, and felt the massive stone give way without any resistance.

The stone swiveled inward.

Revealing a clear tunnel of obsidian.

CHAPTER THIRTY-FOUR

TOM SWITCHED ON his flashlight and swam through the opening.

Genevieve waited on the outside in case something went wrong with the mechanism. It was thousands of years old, after all.

Inside, Tom placed his hands in the exact same position on the sphere, this time closing the door completely from the inside. He took a deep breath, concentrated, and found the same strange grooved indentation on the opposite side of the door.

He repeated the process and the door swiveled open once more.

"We're good," Tom said. "Let's see where it leads."

"All right." Genevieve glanced up above, where the Zodiac had cut the engine. "Right on time. It looks like we might have company."

Tom followed her gaze.

There were already divers entering the water.

"How do you want to play this?" he asked. "Inside the tunnel or out?"

"Inside. We can keep any number of them at bay inside the tunnel. Out here and outnumbered, we're more likely to get surrounded."

"Agreed."

They swam through the opening and Tom quickly closed the ancient door.

Inside, the tunnel headed upward until it reached a dry landing space. He focused the beam of his flashlight down the tunnel. It looked slightly curved, like it was part of a spiral. Tom glanced at his dive computer. It had an inbuilt Air Quality Particle Counting Meter — the same sort of thing a miner might carry that detects oxygen and carbon dioxide levels, as well as the presence of any number of toxic chemicals or gases. The reading showed seventy-eight percent nitrogen, twenty-one percent oxygen and zero point zero four percent carbon dioxide — or roughly the equivalent ratios found in the normal, breathable, atmosphere. Last, the computer was showing no chemical, radiological, or biological threats.

Tom broke the suction on his full faced dive mask. "The air's safe."

Genevieve followed suit, removing her weight belt, dive tank, and flippers. "Good. I really wasn't all that keen on walking to the center of the labyrinth with our SCUBA gear."

They removed their MP5 submachineguns.

The weapons were used by elite forces around the world specifically for their reliability after water submersion. One could leave a loaded MP5 in a 44-gallon drum of water for a month, come back, pick it up and fire all thirty rounds without a single misfire.

Tom set the ambidextrous selector to F — for fully automatic.

And waited for their enemies to come.

CHAPTER THIRTY-FIVE

T HEY WAITED A full hour.

Tom felt his heart race. His breathing was uneven, his concentration fixed, and his jaw set. He and Genevieve had their MP5 submachineguns ready to fire. But the obsidian door never opened.

She said, "Looks like they're not coming."

Tom considered that and shrugged. "Or they're waiting us out?"

Genevieve lowered her MP5. "Or they're waiting us out. Either way, we need to keep going."

"Agreed."

With their diving equipment dumped on the dry ledge of the tunnel, they made their way toward the center of the labyrinth.

The obsidian passageway meandered in an alternating series of curves, forming adjoining spirals. Tom shined the beam of his flashlight in both directions, checking for signs of other people. There were none. For all he knew, they were the first to enter the labyrinth since 1975. His eyes searched the mysterious ebony colored, glassy walls of the tunnel for any sign or purpose — they were entirely blank.

He checked his compass.

They were heading in a generally northern direction.

Tom and Genevieve continued for another twenty minutes.

All the time the tunnel seemed to keep curving inward to the left, before it angled sharply to the right, opening up to a new spiral. He glanced at his compass again. They were headed south, but that didn't matter. They were in a labyrinth. He'd seen plenty of labyrinths since he was kid. It didn't matter what direction you were heading. The path could turn back on itself and turn around again.

He put down the compass.

There was no need for it. Unlike a maze which had complex branching multicursal paths to choose from and was designed to disorient and confuse its users, a labyrinth, by definition was unicursal with a single path to the center, and one entrance that doubled as an exit. A labyrinth was unambiguous with no navigational challenge.

His mind returned to the oldest purpose of a labyrinth — to protect something of value at its center.

A would-be thief might attempt to steal a prize at the center, but it would be extremely difficult to try and escape from it, because the entire process takes so much time.

It was nearly thirty minutes before they reached the center of the labyrinth.

Tom rounded the end of the spiral, which then turned in the opposite direction like one giant horseshoe, before opening up to a large domed vault — not a vault, a perfect sphere — with a diameter of fifty feet.

An obsidian bridge stretched across the room, revealing the levels of the sphere below. A single set of obsidian stairs led all the way from the base to the ceiling in an ascending spiral that hugged the natural curvature of the spherical room.

Tom and Genevieve stepped onto the bridge.

He ran his eyes across the empty walls, sweeping them with the beam of his flashlight in giant swathes from end to end. The light reflected vividly off the walls like a giant mirror.

Tom scrunched up his face, tasting the disappointment,

spreading his hands. "I don't get it. Elise told you the place was left in its original form after the raid in 1975…"

"But it's clearly been wiped clean."

The ground beneath them dropped suddenly with a jolt, maybe an inch or two. Not much. Their weight appeared to have caused it to descend. He listened to a series of mechanical cogs grinding together as the bridge continued its descent.

They glanced at each other. Stay or go?

"Stay," Tom said, defiantly.

"Okay, we stay," Genevieve replied, cradling her MP5 in defense.

The obsidian bridge slowly made its way to the bottom of the sphere. At the epicenter of the sphere, a pedestal now rose in contrast to the bridge, eventually coming to rest at a height of approximately three feet.

Nothing happened for two or three seconds.

There was a distinctive clicking sound and everything changed.

Something flashed in Tom's eyes. He shook his head and tried to blink away the incredulity of his vision.

His eyes narrowed and he swallowed hard. "What the hell is that?"

CHAPTER THIRTY-SIX

T HE SPHERE FILLED with a blue unnatural glow.
Tom had seen the same technology used in one of the previous Master Builder temples. The weighted pedestal had triggered some sort of UV light, which now projected across the walls of the entire sphere, causing thousands of ancient markings to phosphoresce in a myriad of colors. Pictographs came alive in hues of blue, green, purple, and red.

Genevieve's eyes were already raking the strange language. She squinted as she examined the closest pictograph. There was a slight furrow in her forehead, but she remained silent.

"What is it?" Tom asked.

"I can't read this."

"But you grew up in Russia. I thought you could read the language?"

"I can," she said, glancing at another set of unusual writings. "But this isn't Russian."

"It isn't?"

"Now."

Tom ran his hands through his hair. "Okay, but Elise definitely said it was a Russian terrorist cult that was working in here, making no reference to the Master Builders."

"That's right," Genevieve confirmed. "Elise said the writings were definitely Russian."

Tom knew Elise didn't make mistakes. She was robotic in her accuracy. She dealt pedantically with exact names, events, figures, and locations. Therefore, the terrorist group was Russian and they were making written notes in the Russian language.

Ergo, all they needed to do was find those notes.

Tom let out a sigh. "All right, so let's find it then."

All in total, it took another fifteen minutes to locate the mess of garbled Russian text. It was made using local quartz, which etched the writings into the softer obsidian. That explained why they hadn't picked it up at first. The fluorescent pictographs and ancient texts—presumably written by the Master Builders—stood out in the UV light, whereas the white etchings became more concealed.

The various styles of texts spiraled their way up the sphere with the lower levels all pictographs, followed by the indecipherable codex of the Master Builders, and eventually, along the upper sections were Russian scripts etched and superimposed on the original ancient language. The entire sphere was speckled with the various texts, with one exception—roughly two thirds of the way along the ceiling was a small section, maybe a few feet in diameter that appeared conspicuously vacant.

Tom asked, "What do you think happened there?"

Genevieve shrugged. She wasn't an archeologist and was never fond of guessing. "Beats me. Maybe they finished their project? Who knows."

"Okay. Where do you want to start?"

"There!" She fixed the beam of her flashlight on a space about halfway up the wall of the sphere. "That's the lowest section with any Russian text. So, let's start at the beginning."

Tom nodded. It seemed like the best plan.

Genevieve climbed the first eleven steps up the spiral staircase. She studied the inscription. A wry smile formed on her supple lips. "That's strange."

Tom kept his eyes focused on the tunnel through which they had entered. The last thing he wanted was to get caught off guard. "What?"

"The first note refers to something called the Phoenix Plague."

"Okay," Tom said, still not really following. "Does it say what that is?"

"No, but it does make a reference to recommencing the project and then a date — 1434 — two years before the Solovetsky monastery was built!"

"That can't be a coincidence."

"No, but I can't see the connection yet, either."

Tom suppressed a smile. "I don't suppose any of the terrorists were connected to the monastery?"

She shook her head. "Not that we know of."

"All right, let's keep going."

Genevieve nodded and climbed a few more stairs to the next note. Tom left her to make her own notes. There were a lot of markings throughout the sphere and if they stopped to discuss each one of them it might increase the difficulty of an already time-consuming process. Better, he figured, that she made her translations and then they sat down together to discuss their meaning.

While she worked, Tom carefully made a digital recording of the entire sphere. He had no doubt that Sam or Elise would be able to find some sort of useful information from the Master Builder's texts.

Directly above him he spotted a small, almost round section of ceiling with no words on it. He kept his flashlight focused on the blank space and said, "Hey Genevieve, what do you make of this?"

She looked across from where she was on the staircase and said, "Maybe they ran out of things to write about? Who knows, the Master Builders were a people from long ago. Sam and Elise profess to understand them, but I certainly don't."

"All right, I'll take some more pictures, see what Sam and Elise think of it once they get a chance."

Genevieve fixed her flashlight up toward the upper section of the dome. "There's some more Russian text there, but I can't get close enough to read it."

Tom glanced at the twin obsidian stairwells. One on each side of the sphere, each one leading the way from the base to the ceiling in an opposite direction, ascending like a spiral that hugged the natural curvature of the spherical room, right up to the apex.

There were fine marks throughout the dome which suggested something had scraped along the wall at one time or another.

Were there another set of stairs?"

The two staircases were joined by the base of the obsidian orb at the center of the sphere. Tom studied the strange pedestal for a moment.

There were multiple pictograms that meant nothing to him.

At the base was one shaped like a cloud with three human figures floating above. He pressed the cold ornament, which moved inward.

A moment later, the entire staircase lifted an inch off the ground, levitating. It could have been achieved through magnets, or machinery, or some type of ancient technology long forgotten. Tom didn't know and didn't care.

He just needed to work out how to move the stairs.

"Can you please come down here, Genevieve. I think we might be able to move the platform."

"Sure."

Genevieve stepped down with the brisk athleticism of a gymnast.

She stepped off the last stair.

Tom said, "I pressed something over there on the orb and now the entire thing has shifted off the ground. I'm hoping we can move it."

"Only one way to find out. Let's try."

She leaned against the base of the step before Tom could do anything, and the entire thing moved. There was no strain in her muscular physique.

"Wow! Superwoman!" Tom said.

"I'm barely touching it."

Tom put his hands on the side of the stairs, gripping them for support. "Okay, you head up there, and tell me when the stairs align at the spot you were trying to study."

Genevieve moved up the stairs as fast as she had come down them.

Two thirds of the way up, she said, "Keep going. Another five or six feet."

Tom pushed gently, and the stairs swung round on an invisible axis.

"Stop!" Genevieve yelled.

Tom continued searching the area, filming every aspect of the room as best he could.

About ten minutes later, Genevieve said, "You'd better come up here, Tom!"

He glanced at her face, where small lines of fear developed beneath her eyes. "What is it?"

"I think we have a serious problem!"

CHAPTER THIRTY-SEVEN

G ENEVIEVE SAID, "THEY'VE been genetically modifying the human genome for centuries... possibly even millennia!"

"How?" Tom asked. "Why? I don't understand. For what purpose?"

"How would you alter a person's genetics prior to modern medicine and DNA sequence editing?"

"Hi, I'm Tom," he said, holding his hand out sarcastically. "An expert cave diver and pilot. I'm not sure why you think I know anything about gene editing."

She shook her head dismissively, as though he was over-thinking things. "How does natural biology and evolution work?"

"Information regarding what works and what didn't work gets passed on by those who survive."

"Right. Darwin's theory of evolution."

"What's this got to do with ancient technology, terrorism, and Ben Gellie's parents?"

"What if you wanted to create a very specific genetic trait, but despite not having the science, you have time. How would you do it?"

"Through breeding?" Tom asked.

"Right. The Russian cult translated and read the ancient scripts left here by the Master Builders. They couldn't work out the science, but they had a genetic recipe..."

"For what?"

"I don't know, but look at this." Genevieve read some more text in Russian, then expelled a deep breath of air and swallowed hard.

"What is it?" Tom asked.

"Some of the text is missing. But, if I'm reading this right, they were making a weapon—the Phoenix Plague."

"The Phoenix Plague?" Tom repeated the name. "As in the mythological bird that kept burning only to rise again from its ashes?"

"That would be the one," she replied.

"How?" Tom asked.

"I don't know."

"They were trying to create a deadly virus! A plague capable of destroying the world, so that what, something else could rise from the ashes of human remains?"

"It looks like it," Genevieve admitted.

"But who?"

Genevieve shook her head. "It doesn't say."

Tom fixed his flashlight on the last section, the very ending of all the writings. "There's something else! What does it say?"

"You're not going to believe it."

"What?"

"They weren't just trying to develop a deadly virus. They succeeded in developing it, incubating it into a deadly host, genetically designed, to be a ticking time bomb, capable of releasing the virus onto the world in the most effective way possible."

"Where?"

"It doesn't say. But it gives the name of the host..."

Tom shouted, "Who?"

Genevieve swallowed hard. "Ben Gellie."

CHAPTER THIRTY-EIGHT

TOM'S EYES WERE wide, his chest pounding at the news. "Are you certain?"

"Yeah," she replied, her eyes cast downward, fixated on the Russian text next to the ancient Master Builder script. "There are words missing and things I'll need to check on the computer tablet, but I think it's clear, Ben Gellie is a deadly terrorist, who's about to bring the human race to its knees."

"Sam was certain Ben was one of the good guys."

Genevieve shrugged. "It might be true, even."

"How can you believe that when you think he's the one carrying the Phoenix Plague?"

"Maybe he doesn't know the truth. He's just the host, a carrier of a disease he doesn't yet know exists. He's no more evil than a weapon, which has no say over how it's used."

"All right," Tom said, realizing that what she was saying was probably the truth. "What do we know exactly?"

"Okay, like I said, there are words missing."

"Why?"

Her well-trimmed eyebrow arched. "Why what?"

Tom said, "Why are there words missing?"

"I don't know. There have been missing parts throughout all the Russian notes. It might be text that has faded over time, or it was written and then washed off after discovering it was wrong…"

"Or someone intentionally removed it?" Tom suggested.

"Like redacting a secret document?"

"We can't rule it out."

Genevieve made a dramatic sigh. "No. But whatever the case, those words are gone. All we have to work with is what we've got."

"So what have we got?" Tom asked.

"There's a story about John and Jenny coming together as the perfect genetic match to develop a host with the strength to survive the Phoenix Plague long enough to complete its incubation period."

"Maybe John and Jenny had another child?"

"Maybe, but this one specifically refers to Ben."

"You're kidding me!"

Genevieve's face crunched up in fear. "Afraid not. It refers to three ancient strains of DNA used to achieve the goal. It then lists those as: *Australopithecus boisei, Homo ergaster,* and *Homo neanderthalensis.*"

Tom turned his palms upward. "That's it? I don't get it. I thought you said it specifically refers to Ben."

"It does," Genevieve replied, her voice emphatic. "Did you ever study biology?"

"A little in high school. Nothing that's coming to mind right now."

"Good thing I paid attention in school then. In biology, a tribe is a taxonomic rank above genus, but below family and subfamily. Bring back memories?"

"Not a thing."

"All right. In biological classification, taxonomic rank is the relative level of a group of organisms in a taxonomic hierarchy. Although the system is constantly being updated, there are currently eight ranks widely accepted for classifying all living things. Starting from the top down, these are domain, kingdom, phylum, class, order, family, genus, species." Genevieve leveled her eyes at him. "Now do you remember?"

"Briefly. Go on."

"At the highest level, domain separates all life into three classes, Archaea, Bacteria, and Eukarya. Humans for example, fall under the domain Eukarya. Humans fall under the kingdom of Animalia, the phylum of Chordata, class of mammal, order of primates, family of Hominidae, genus of Homo, and species of *sapiens*."

"Genevieve!" Tom yelled. "Get to the point!"

"Australopithecus and Homo are both part of the family of hominidae. Australopithecus boisei, Homo ergaster, and Homo neanderthalensis all lived during the same period roughly a hundred thousand years ago and some of their DNA is still carried in humans today."

"Okay, so you're saying John and Jenny Gellie have ancient DNA in their blood?"

Genevieve took a deep breath and said, "I'm saying, the magic formula included *boisei, ergaster,* and *neanderthal* DNA — B.E.N."

"Ah Christ!" Tom said. "Ben Gellie is the product of genetic engineering! He's the carrier of the Phoenix Plague. We need to leave now! We need to get a message to Sam — he's got it all wrong."

They both started to run up the stairs, racing for the main obsidian tunnel. Once there, they ran at full speed for nearly fifteen minutes, racing through the series of mind numbing spirals that seemed intent on stopping their progress.

The tunnel curved left and they entered the final spiral and dropped to the floor — as the thunderous echo of shots raked the wall above, sending fragments and fine shards of obsidian glass splintering onto their backs, announcing the springing of a trap.

CHAPTER THIRTY-NINE

G ENEVIEVE GOT A shot off before she hit the ground.
She squeezed the trigger automatically and her MP5 submachinegun became a natural extension of her arm. By the time her shoulders crashed into the cold, obsidian floor, she'd released five shots, killing two men.

Tom stood up, his weapon raised, ready to fire. Both remained silent, their eyes darting between each other and the two bodies.

Genevieve listened.

She heard the sound of blood pounding in the back of her head, the inhale and exhale of her own labored breathing, the slight click as Tom changed his weapon to F—for fully automatic fire—but she didn't hear any footsteps.

The tunnel was quiet. Deathly so.

She moved farther along the spiral, keeping her senses focused on the open space up ahead. The tunnel was empty, the walls of obsidian providing no cover and limited camouflage. Tom moved with her. Neither spoke. They didn't have to. They were experts in this sort of field, and lovers, making them work with the innate harmony that transcended verbal communication.

Tom bent down and glanced at two bodies. He didn't check a pulse. They both had two 9mm bullet strikes their heads. No one was going to survive those shots. Instead, he ran his eyes across the two men, rolled them over.

Genevieve glanced at him. "Well?"

"No insignia, no ID, carrying Israeli Uzi submachineguns."

"Mercenaries. The question is who's paying? The US Defense Department or someone private?"

Tom said, "We're not going to find out staying here."

She heard the sound of dozens of footsteps running. "We're not going to remain alive staying here! Let's retreat to the next spiral change."

"Agreed!"

Genevieve ran a hundred or so feet until she reached the point where the spiral changed direction, opening to a new branch of the labyrinth.

She stopped at that point. They had the advantage of some decent cover, while the advancing mercenaries were out in the open.

They both aimed their weapons down the curving tunnel. At least ten mercenaries came into view all at once.

Genevieve and Tom opened fire.

Their shots ripped the first wave of their opponents to pieces. She and Tom spaced out their shots so that at any stage one of them still had a near full magazine at the ready.

She felt the unique calm of battle.

Breathing deeply, she traced the fallen mercenaries. One of them, with a sucking chest wound, moved for his Uzi and she put two bullets in his skull.

The obsidian labyrinth became silent.

It lasted nearly five minutes. An eternity during a firefight in an enclosed battlespace.

Then someone threw something metal into the tunnel.

Thick smoke billowed from the green M18 colored smoke grenades. It quickly filled the labyrinth, forming an impenetrable visual screen.

Genevieve felt Tom squeeze her arm. She understood what it meant — we need to retreat. She nodded. They ran back through the spiral until they reached the next opposing turn. There they set up for their attackers once more.

Tom said, "We can't hold them off here indefinitely."

"That's great. You got a better idea?"

"Yeah, let's find another way out!"

Her lips curled with incredulity. "What have you got in mind? We're inside a labyrinth. By definition, that means one way in and out!"

He met her eye. "Elise said that during the CIA's attack on the terrorist group, they slaughtered everyone, but somehow John and Jenny Gellie escaped?"

"That's right. Unaware of the US elite military presence in the labyrinth, the rest of their cult was massacred by superior forces."

"So John and Jenny Gellie weren't inside at the time of the attack?"

"No. There's video footage that shows them entering the labyrinth. They were the ringleaders."

"Then how the hell did they get out?" Tom asked, with a rueful grin.

"Good question." Genevieve thought about that for a moment. "There must be a secret escape passage."

"The monastery!"

"What?"

"You said work on the Solovetsky monastery commenced in 1436, but the monks had gathered in the area, declaring it sacred land, nearly two years earlier!"

"That's right…" Genevieve confirmed, not yet sure where he was going with it.

"What if someone knew about the labyrinth?" Tom asked. "What if someone knew exactly where it came out, but the raised sea level meant that they could no longer access it?"

"What are you saying?"

Tom said, "I think the Solovetsky monks bored a tunnel into the sphere, dropping down from there. Maybe it was an accident or maybe someone amongst them descended from the Master Builders and knew the truth? Either way, once they found the sphere, they set a course to follow the ancient scripts and produce the Phoenix Plague."

"But Bolshoi Zayatsky's nearly two miles from the Solovetsky fortified monastery!"

"Is it?" Tom's eyes narrowed. "How would we know? That's the purpose of a labyrinth: to confuse its intruders. Maybe, all along, we've been making our way north, into the grounds beneath the monastery."

The first group of mercenaries came into view, hugging the edge of the obsidian spiral.

Genevieve opened fire with her MP5.

The first two fell, and the third emptied his full 32 round magazine toward them. Genevieve ducked behind the corner of the spiral.

She felt a fresh shiver. "We're never going to outgun them. Let's try and find your secret tunnel."

Tom grinned. "I think I already know where it is."

"You do?"

"Yeah. That blank spot at the top of the dome. The one without any writings!"

"Of course!"

They ran all the way back to the sphere.

Tom climbed down the stairs and up to the orb at the center. Genevieve fixed her flashlight on the raised pictograms.

Behind them, she heard the heavy breathing of people running hard.

They were getting close.

Tom said, "None of these markings look anything like a trap door."

Genevieve pointed to a pictograph that had a single circle inside a circle. "It's that one!"

"You're sure?"

"No. But I've seen a similar description on the side of the Great Pyramid of Giza, where the secret escape passage used to be."

Tom closed his eyes, trying to picture the symbol at the base of the Khufu's tomb. "You're right!"

Genevieve pressed the stone. Unseen mechanisms started to move above. She climbed the stairs and fired several rounds down the obsidian tunnel as a warning to the mercenaries.

They reached the top of the obsidian dome.

The ceiling seemed perfectly solid. There were no cracks. No sign of any potential opening. Genevieve pushed on it, but nothing budged.

The wall beside them sparked as bullets ripped into the ancient volcanic stone.

Genevieve turned and opened up return fire.

Tom turned the butt of his Heckler and Koch upward and struck the ceiling. The outer layer of obsidian fractured under the force, splintering into multiple pieces and falling through to the ground nearly fifty feet below.

Genevieve tilted her head upward.

An internal ladder was carved into the stone.

"Go!" she shouted. "I'm right behind you."

Tom nodded and disappeared into the void above.

She emptied the last of her rounds into the tunnel below and then followed Tom into the escape passage.

Climbing hand over hand, she made her way quickly to the top of the narrow chimney. It opened into a concealed vestibule of the stone cathedral.

A monk glanced at them, recognition and fear displayed across his face in abject horror at the location from which they had come.

Regaining his composure, the monk looked at them, and said, "What have you done?"

They pushed past him, running out through the nave into an under-cover passageway.

Behind them, she heard the monk shout, "Quick! They're getting away."

Genevieve imagined her pursuers climbing the secret passage. They would be swarming out of the cathedral any minute.

She and Tom reached a conflux of three separate hallways.

"Which way?" Tom asked.

"Go left!"

They ran through the refectory and into the open courtyard.

Up ahead, someone had had the good sense to close the gates.

Shots fired from behind them.

Tom returned fire with a couple short bursts.

Genevieve started to climb the bell tower. At thirty feet, she jumped across to the fortified masonry wall that surrounded the monastery.

Tom was racing up the tower behind her.

She loaded her last magazine into her submachinegun and provided him with cover fire. A monk ordered them to stop. But both sides kept firing.

Genevieve ran along the top of the masonry wall.

At the end of the western wall stood the guard tower, where a monk had triumphantly closed the gate. Already, he was now in the process of trying to open it again.

Genevieve pointed her MP5 at him and shouted in Russian, "Don't you dare!"

The monk put his hands skyward in supplication.

She grabbed the rope used to raise and lower the gate. Tom pushed past the monk, who quickly moved out of his way.

A group of monks armed with rudimentary weapons, interspersed with the remaining mercenaries, were now racing toward them.

Tom gripped the rope with one arm.

Shots raked the rampart, sending medieval masonry splintering into a torrent of shards. Genevieve grabbed the rope just below Tom's hand and they simultaneously swung over the thirty-three-foot fortified buttress.

Reaching the muddy ground below, they ran toward the Beriev Be-103 Bekas amphibious seaplane. It must have been how the mercenaries got to the island.

The cockpit door was open and the pilot was having a smoke at the end of the jetty. He turned around, took one look at Genevieve and Tom and dived into the icy water.

Genevieve climbed into the cockpit through the raised bifold winged doors. Tom untied the aircraft from the jetty and gave it a gentle push off as he climbed in, pulling the hatches shut behind him.

She shoved the red fuel mixture throttle to full, switched the master electrics to on, gave the primer three quick depressions, and flicked the ignition key. The twin propellers started to spin. She glanced at her position in relation to the jetty. Already the current had pulled her out.

With her right hand on the throttle, she eased it all the way forward until the twin engines whined with joy.

She turned out to sea and the little seaplane picked up speed.

Behind them she heard the steady staccato of UZIs being fired, but already, the aircraft was increasing the distance between them.

The fuselage hydroplaned, skipping enthusiastically across Prosperity Bay.

Genevieve pulled the wheel firmly toward her chest and the

aircraft took off into the air. She brought the aircraft round in a large circuit, being sure to keep enough space between the monastery and them.

She expelled a deep breath of air. They had made it.

That's where the reprieve ended, because Tom picked up his satellite phone and reminded her that all their troubles were only just starting.

And her mind returned to their earlier discovery...

They needed Sam to know Ben Gellie was the host of the Phoenix Plague.

CHAPTER FORTY

MINNESOTA RAILWAY LINE

T HE FREIGHT TRAIN cruised at nearly eighty miles per hour along the class five railway tracks.

Inside his opulent shipping container, Sam Reilly heard his Nokia 3110C start to ring. He rolled off the couch, unsure what time it was, and answered on the third ring. "Hello?"

"Sam!" It was Tom's voice, and he could hear the relief behind the gravel.

"You okay, Tom?"

"Sure. I'm just a bit relieved to know that you're alive. Are you all right?"

Sam glanced out through the digital window, where Lake Superior could be seen in the distance. He smiled. "Never better."

"Good. Are you…" the phone started to break up.

Sam moved to the other side of the shipping container, as though that might improve his chance of getting some decent reception.

"You there, Tom?" he asked.

"Ben's not…"

"I can't hear you, Tom. What did you find at Bolshoi Zayatsky

Island?"

Through the garbled hiss of his outdated cell phone he heard the words, "…Phoenix Plague."

"What the hell's the Phoenix Plague?"

"Did you hear me, Sam?"

"No. I'm having trouble getting reception. Look if I cut out, I'll call you from North Dakota…"

He glanced at his phone.

It had stopped working altogether. He looked at the screen. It was dark. The damned thing had run out of batteries. He didn't even have a charger for it. It was another twenty dollars, and he didn't have the money to buy one at the general store at Harpers Ferry. He cursed himself for not getting Elise to supply him with a modern smartphone.

Ben looked at him. "Everything all right?"

"Yeah. That was my friend. He's just been to Bolshoi Zayatsky Island."

Ben's eyes widened. "Did he find anything?"

"I don't know. My cell phone died before he could finish telling me about it."

"What did he say?"

"Something about the Phoenix Plague."

Ben's lips curled into a wry smile. "Is that all?"

"Yeah. Ever heard of the Phoenix Plague?"

Ben shook his head. "No. But it can't be good."

CHAPTER FORTY-ONE

O'HARE AIRPORT, CHICAGO, ILLINOIS

"WE JUST FOUND him!" Ryan Devereaux said.

The man at the check-in table handed him his boarding pass. "I'm sorry sir, you're going to need to turn that off before you board."

Ryan looked up and stopped. He was the last one to board his flight. Once on board there was nothing he could do to manage the arrest. He held his cell phone to his ear and met the steward's eye defiantly. "I said, just a minute."

On the other end of the line, the Secretary of Defense asked, "Where?"

He lowered his voice. "In a shipping container on his way to Minot, North Dakota!"

"How'd you work that one out?"

"Tom just changed his flight plan on his route back from Russia. He's now heading direct to North Dakota. Also, we hacked his computer, and found him checking a third party dummy company—most likely owned by Sam Reilly—which purchased a readymade shipping-container-come-tiny home in Frederick and had it shipped to North Dakota."

"How did Sam and Ben get inside?"

"Here's the good bit. I contacted the logistics company, who told me that the purchaser requested it to be shipped by road to Martinsburg before being put on a freight train to Minot!"

"Good God!" The Secretary said. "That's them!"

"What are you going to do?"

"I have an undercover team of agents and SWAT converging at the railway yards at Minot. I'm about to board a flight to North Dakota to oversee the operation personally. We're going to catch him this time."

"You'd better. We both know what's riding on this."

"It will all work this time. One thing's bothering me though."

The Secretary said, "What?"

"They're close to the Canadian border, so why stop there?" Devereaux gestured one finger to the steward and mouthed the words, *just one more second!* "It means that they're heading somewhere specific. The question is what's in Minot, North Dakota, that Sam and Ben need?"

"Not what. Who. And I know why, too." The Secretary audibly exhaled. "This has just upped the ante."

Devereaux raised his eyebrows. "Who?"

He felt a shiver of terror at her response.

"Aliana Wolfgang."

CHAPTER FORTY-TWO

MINOT, NORTH DAKOTA

A LIANA WOLFGANG GLANCED out her window.

It had started to snow. Yesterday's fog had become today's powdery snowflakes, drifting down lazily in the still air. The weather forecasts were warning people about the blizzard of the year, if not the decade. Schools weren't closed yet, but every single TV station, radio station, and schoolchild was predicting heavy snowfall—the sort of blizzard that brings a place like Minot to a standstill.

The temperature was twenty degrees Fahrenheit, cold but not *too* cold. You'd want to put your heavy coat on, that was for sure, but you didn't need to put your light coat on underneath your heavy coat. Wind chill? Without any wind, there wasn't any. No, the storm hadn't arrived yet. They might still have another day of reprieve before it hit.

Aliana ignored the weather warnings.

Her mind was fixated on one of the greatest leads of her career in pharmaceutical research and development. It would be the greatest advancement in life expectancy, quality of life, and medicine in her lifetime. Commercially, it would make her company more valuable than gold. She smiled, revealing a set of white evenly spaced teeth.

It made her think of that song by Queen—*Who Wants to Live*

Forever?

She'd heard the song plenty of times in her teens. Queen might have had some insight that she was missing, but the honest answer to the question was always going to be a resounding, *everyone wants to live forever!*

And her new research might pave the way to one day give it to them.

Her cell phone rang. She wanted to ignore it. Right now, she had no interest in talking to anyone. Her mind was fixed on both the scientific and ethical dilemma she'd been given.

She glanced at her smartphone. The name came up from her directory—Emma. They were at MIT together. While Aliana studied microbiology and biomedicine, Emma studied straight medicine. Two years ago, she inherited her father's pharmaceutical company. They had often talked about what the two companies could do working together, with Aliana's performing the research and development, while Emma's produced and distributed the product.

Her heart skipped a beat. She pressed accept. "Emma!"

"Aliana," replied Emma. "Did you get the sample I sent you?"

"Yes."

There was a brief silence. "You want to tell me what you think of it?"

Aliana expelled a deep breath. She'd known Emma for most of her adult life. Still it amazed her that her friend had entrusted her with the blood sample. It was like mailing the winning lotto ticket to a friend to photocopy before you cash it in. "All right, it might be the breakthrough of the century. Where did you get it?"

"A prisoner having routine blood tests."

"Does he know he has the genetic mutation?"

"Not a clue."

"Christ!" Aliana swore. "Do you know how many laws we're

breaking?"

"Does it matter?" Emma's voice was flat, her response anything but flippant. The potential rewards from their discovery had the chance to change the world and save lives. It was the very reason they had both gotten into their industries: to help people.

"You're right, something like this, there are no risks too great to take the chance. It's too valuable."

Emma's voice hardened. "So, can you reverse engineer the mutation?"

"I don't know yet. Everything's possible."

In ten years, they *might* be able to prevent most types of cancer. That alone was worth whatever she sacrificed. In her research, she had known so many people who had only met her because they had fallen under the shadow of the terrible disease. And she had known so many of them who had since died...

Emma said, "We analyzed the DNA on one of the previous samples. There was definitely no sign of a breakdown along the telomeres."

Carefully, Aliana said, "No sign?"

"None," Emma replied. "Now, I'm not one of the world's top DNA researchers. But even I know how unusual that is."

It was. The shortening of the telomeres at the ends of DNA strands, not just in human beings but in almost every living species on the planet, was one of nature's tradeoffs. The telomeres were, as far as they could currently ascertain, a bunch of meaningless junk at the ends of each strand of DNA as it weaved its way into a double helix.

Aliana thought about that in silence for a moment, because even those long sequences of meaningless junk had a purpose.

Every time a living being needed to reproduce its DNA in order to replace and rejuvenate the cells in its body, the bodily systems in charge of the reproduction "snipped" off a short section of that junk code.

Why?

As the telomeres became shorter and shorter, the valuable code of the DNA past the sections of telomeres became more and more exposed. Finally, the DNA became shortened enough that the cells weren't able to reproduce, and therefore replace, damaged cells.

Aging.

The loss of the telomeres was a countdown to aging...and death.

But without the destruction of the telomeres came a second, even more serious issue: mutation. The earth was constantly being bombarded with solar radiation, despite the protection of the earth's ozone layer. Life was always encountering *something* that damaged its cells on a molecular level. Chemicals, radiation, random chance...

Some of the mutations improved the gene pool; others ensured that it ended before it could reproduce.

Over a long enough period of time, though, DNA *would* be mutated into something undesirable.

Cancer.

By guaranteeing individual cells could only reproduce so long before they wiped themselves out, nature protected itself against most of the mutations that would lead to cancer—most of the time.

Cancer, however, fought back—by forcing cells to produce telomerase, an enzyme that added more telomeres right back on to the ends of the DNA. One of the most famous lines of cancer cells, that of Henrietta Lacks, or the HeLa line, was practically immortal, because of the way it aggressively produced telomerase.

So the fact that the prisoner's cell sample wasn't losing telomeres as it reproduced wasn't exactly unique. Unless...

"In a healthy individual?" she asked.

"No sign of cancer. None."

"Telomerase levels?"

"They were completely normal."

She drummed her fingers on the tabletop and took another sip of coffee. "That doesn't necessarily mean anything." In some types of cancer, telomerase levels didn't rise at all.

She thought about it some more, pulling her coffee close to her chest and letting the steam waft up into her nose. "How old is the subject?"

"Forty. He looks thirty."

"Have you met him?" she asked.

"Yes."

"What's he like?"

"Handsome, polite. Currently a threat to national security."

Aliana grinned. "There's always something, isn't there?"

Emma's voice softened. "I'll say. I'm not kidding. The guy seemed really nice."

Aliana's eyebrows narrowed with disapproval. "What did he do?"

"I don't know."

"You didn't ask?"

Emma said, "No. I'm a medical doctor. I treat who I'm asked to treat. That's all."

The lines around Aliana's face hardened. Something about Emma's voice sent a chill down her spine. Had she just been lied to?

It brought her back to the original question… *was there a crime so morally and ethically wrong that she shouldn't commit it in order to give the new drug a chance to change the world?*

It came back again with a resounding, *no.*

"All right, I'll keep at it," Aliana said. "Look. If we're going to do this we're going to have to do it right. That will mean dipping into some significant capital. I'm okay with that, but I don't honestly think the company will have the resources that you're talking about, both in expertise and material, to reverse engineer the sample you've given me."

Emma said, "I agree. I've been thinking the same thing."

"And?"

"I think we should merge the two companies. Pool our assets. I'm willing to put everything on the table to make this happen."

Aliana admitted, "I don't even know how we would go about such a merger."

"We can talk deals soon. I've told the hospital I'm not coming in for the rest of the week. I'll be on a flight to meet up with you as soon as I can."

"Both companies are publically listed. A merger will require some government oversight. And more time."

"You'll see," Emma said. "There are structures in place that would trigger a merger, if it's warranted or necessary. But for the most part, it's nothing but shared profit and shared opportunity. And the chance to cure cancer."

It was an overblown phrase. Cancer researchers never thought in terms of "curing cancer." It was impossible, too big to hope for. You might as well hope for the sun to stop shining, because that's what it would take to end all mutations.

And where would humanity be without mutations?

Still in the trees with the rest of the monkeys?

No, without mutations, life didn't exist. There *was* no cure for cancer.

But there might be a cure for *some* types of cancer. Or…a way to stop cells that weren't cancerous from aging.

Take your pick.

Aliana said, "When will you get here?"

Emma said, "I'll be on a flight first thing in the morning."

CHAPTER FORTY-THREE

DEVILS LAKE, NORTH DAKOTA—ONE A.M.

T HE TRAIN ROLLED on through the night.

Sam stayed awake, having slept intermittently for the previous twenty-four hours. He was recharged, ready for whatever came next. He listened to the drone of the train's wheels, monotonously grinding along the iron track, the freight cart rocking gently, reminding him of the swell of a gentle ocean.

Ben jammed himself into a ball on the adjoining, two-seater couch. He joined the sleep of the damned after refusing to sleep for the first leg of the trip, in case the train was boarded. Sam checked his watch, they were getting close.

The train started to slow. He glanced out the digital window.

A sign read, *Welcome to Devils Lake.*

Sam grabbed his thick jacket and woke up Ben. "Wake up. This is our stop."

Ben tried to withhold a yawn. His lips curled into what might pass for a smile. "This is Minot?"

"No. Devil's Lake."

Ben blinked, his mind trying to place them in relation to Minot. He opened up the map. "It says on the map here that the next stop is Rugby and then Minot."

"That sounds right."

"We want to get to Minot, right?"

"Right."

"So why are we getting off at Devil's lake?"

"Because there's still a chance THEY know where we're headed."

"You said everything was purchased through a separate business, not connected to you in any way?"

"Sure. But like you said, they're the government; they're not playing by the same rules as you and I. Which means, they might just know where we're headed." Sam pointed to Minot on the map. "If they do, they'll have a small army of law enforcement officers waiting for us here, and if I was Devereaux, I'd put a second group at Rugby, just in case we get off early."

"So we're getting off two stations back?"

Sam grinned. "So we're getting off two stations back."

The train reached its stop with a slight jolt. Sam opened the shipping container's door and he and Ben slipped through. He closed the door, making sure it was still locked, and stepped off the track, into the shade of the riparian forest.

They crouched down and waited until the freight train moved again.

As soon as it left, Sam stepped forward, trying to orient himself. He turned around slowly, his eyes taking in the landscape in the light of the gibbous moon. They were surrounded by thick forests and distant mountains, but there was no sign of a small city.

Ben looked at him. "What is it?"

Sam swallowed hard. "We were supposed to pick up a car left for us at the station at Devils Lake."

"So where is it?"

"I don't know, but judging by the lack of roads and, for that matter, train stations, my guess is our train made an unscheduled stop."

"Great. How far out do you think we are?"

Sam tried to shrug, feigning an indifference he no longer felt. "I have no idea. Hopefully not too far, it's got to be getting down below twenty degrees Fahrenheit. If we don't find shelter soon, we'll freeze to death out here."

Ben sighed heavily. "Then we'd better make a start."

CHAPTER FORTY-FOUR

MINOT RAILWAY STATION, NORTH DAKOTA.

R YAN DEVEREAUX WATCHED the freight train roll in.
His lips curled into the crooked smile of a gambler whose
efforts were about to finally pay off. A pair of military
helicopters hovered directly above the train, their powerful
spotlights and heat sensors making certain no one managed to
open a door and jump off unannounced.

The train engineer brought the cab up to the start of the
platform, applied the airbrakes, and shut down the massive
diesel engines.

He met Devereaux's eye, his jaw set firm. "You mind telling
me what's going on?"

"Yes. An officer here will take you aside for questioning while
we search your train."

The engineer crossed his arms, sticking out his chest, ready to
argue the point, but one glance at the FBI agents and SWAT
team who were all armed to the teeth, and the man simply
nodded and kept walking.

Devereaux depressed the mike on his portable radio. "All
right, move in!"

The FBI agents secured the perimeter around the train, while
the SWAT team cleared the train individual carriage after

carriage. It was a long process, because many of the shipping containers being hauled were locked.

As a consequence, Devereaux's agency racked up a small fortune in intentional damages to property in the process. All told, nearly an hour passed before the entire train was searched and he finally accepted the fact that Sam and Ben were no longer on board.

He picked up his cell phone and dialed the Secretary of Defense's private number.

"Tell me you have him!" she demanded.

"They're not on the train."

"So they got off earlier."

"No. We had people watching at Rugby. No one got on and no one got off."

The Secretary said, "Maybe he's already there. You know what that means?"

Devereaux understood the consequences. Aliana Wolfgang owned a biotech company, theoretically capable of mass replicating Ben Gellie's blood. There was a reason he'd come directly to this spot. Aliana provided him with the means to infect the world.

The muscles in his face stiffened. "I'll stop him, ma'am."

CHAPTER FORTY-FIVE

T HE TEMPERATURE SEEMED to drop quickly.

At least as the thermometer fell, the moisture in the air dissipated, meaning that it had finally stopped snowing. Sam pulled the hood of his thick woolen jacket tighter across his face. What little skin was still visible to the outside extremes now stung from the icy bite. A small snow-covered road led into the forest. There was a solid gate and what looked like a large house round the back.

Ben said, "We should go there, find some sort of shelter before this storm hits."

"They're not going to be happy about meeting a couple of vagrants in the middle of the night. They're likely to call the cops, no matter what story we give them."

Ben shrugged. "We can keep them quiet until we leave."

"Then what?"

"I don't know, but we're going to die if we're still out here when this storm hits!"

Sam mulled that over for a minute. "Do we keep following the tracks or find shelter?"

"Take the damned shelter."

"All right," Sam agreed. "Let's go see what happens."

A sliver of moonlight permeated the heavily forested conifer trees that lined the snow-covered lane. The driveway looked dilapidated, with overgrown branches making it unlikely any cars had driven down the laneway in a number of years.

Sixty feet in, and they were confronted by a large ornamental steel gate that seemed at odds with the rest of their impression of the property.

Sam ran his eyes across the gate, turning his gaze upward, at the fixed security camera. "That seem odd to you?"

"I don't know. Maybe they're not home over winter — hell I know I wouldn't want to be — and so they like to have a security camera to watch over the place. Who knows?"

"You think they're watching us?" Sam asked.

"At four in the morning? No way."

"Yeah, you're probably right."

Sam gripped the fence and climbed over. It was vertical with a series of horizontal arms, making it easy to climb. If he had to guess, it was built to stop vehicles, not people.

Ben followed him over and they continued down toward what appeared to be a large log house. There were no windows to the house at all. It didn't look like it had been boarded up for the winter; instead it appeared as though the entire place had been built with the windows intentionally left out.

"Something seem odd to you about this place?" Sam asked.

"Yeah, everything. The entire place gives me the creeps."

Sam's eyes narrowed. "You want to look for another place to find shelter?"

"No way. Spooky or not, I want to get inside and get warm. I don't see any cars around here. So maybe we got lucky and no one's home."

"All right. You still have those lock picks?"

"Yeah."

"So show me what you can do with this door."

Ben withdrew the two lock picks from his wallet and started to work on the door. It took longer this time. The padlock at the summer camp was straight forward, whereas the door lock was obviously made to a much higher standard.

Sam said, "Can you do it?"

Ben closed his eyes, feeling with his half frozen gloved fingers, instead. "I think so."

"You never told me why you're carrying lock picks."

Ben made a thin-lipped uncomfortable smile. "It's not what it looks like. I'm not interested in breaking and entering."

"Sure," Sam said, in a voice that clearly stated anything but that he believed him.

"I'm serious. I mean, what I do is far from legal, but it's not breaking and entering, in a traditional sense. And it definitely doesn't warrant getting me on the FBI's number one most wanted list of fugitives."

Sam grinned. "All right, so tell me what it is?"

Ben jiggled the pick upward. There was slight shift in the locking mechanism. He held it there and now maneuvered the second one in the opposite direction, searching for the latch.

"It looks like we're going to be here all night; we might even freeze to death in the process, so you may as well tell me."

"Yeah, whatever. None of it matters now. I think it's fairly safe to say I'm never returning to my old life, so I suppose I can come clean."

"What was it?"

"You know I worked for the justice department, right?"

"Right. I think you said that earlier."

"So, politicians from both sides of the divide are constantly lobbied. Every one of them pushing their own agenda, you know what I mean?"

"Sure."

"What if I told you one of those groups boasted the ability to control nearly twenty percent of the senators in Office, meaning that those votes in Congress could be bought?"

Sam shrugged. "I'd say, twenty percent seems a little low, wouldn't you?"

"Haha… very funny. I'd have you know that despite the in-house fighting that the media would lead us to believe, the majority of US senators have spent their lives serving their country, for no other reason than they were compelled by duty."

"Except for the twenty cheats in Office?"

"Even the majority of the cheats as you call them mean well."

Sam lifted his eyebrow with incredulity. "Really?"

"Yeah, that's what makes this organization so dangerous. They target individual senators, find their weaknesses, and apply pressure. Most don't even know they could be bought."

"So where do you come in?"

"Well, the company that does this lobbying. One of its most capable lobbyists is a woman named Jessica Chase."

"Jessica Chase," Sam repeated the name. It meant nothing to him. "What about her?"

Ben's lips curled into a suppressed smile.

Sam asked, "What?"

"Well, I was supposed to have a date with her yesterday…"

"You're kidding me. What were you going to do?"

"I was asked to search her house, see if I could find anything."

"What good would it have been if you did? Wouldn't everything be inadmissible in court, given the means by which it was obtained?"

"Sure, but we're not trying to go to court, not yet anyway. Right now, we're still trying to prove to our bosses that this thing exists."

"Right, so you're sleeping with a girl to get a promotion?"

Ben shrugged. "Something like that."

"I think I liked you better when I thought you were a common thief." Sam chuckled. "At least then you would have unlocked this damned door by now, and we'd be inside getting warm."

Something clicked on the lock.

Ben turned the handle.

The door swung open slightly.

Sam glanced inside. The place was open, like a giant hall. Large overhead lights filled the room with light. There were more than a dozen people working inside. They wore masks and stirred large metal vats that looked like cauldrons. No one looked up.

He closed the door, silently turning the handle into place. He swallowed and said to Ben, "Of all the shitty luck, we had to stumble upon a meth lab!"

CHAPTER FORTY-SIX

SAM WHISPERED, "THAT explains the security cameras and blocked driveway."

Ben nodded. "Yeah, but it doesn't explain how they move the stuff after it's made."

"Who cares? Let's get out of here."

"I care. That lane we came down hasn't been driven on in years. That means they're not shipping the drugs out from there. Ergo, they must have another way in and out. There must have been a dozen or so people working inside, they don't live here, so where are their cars?"

"Not our problem," replied Sam.

"No, but it might be our solution. Cars can't be stored out in the cold in this part of the world. They'll be tucked safely away somewhere nearby. Find the cars, we might just find a way out of here. There must be something round the back."

"It'll be dangerous."

Ben shrugged. "Trying to walk anywhere from here will be deadly, so I'm up for it."

"All right."

They headed past the log-house-come-meth lab following the trail as it split into a fork, with one path leading farther south toward Devils Lake and the other turning into a more easterly direction. Buried within a dense forest of conifer trees, the track to the east became more protected from the elements and better maintained.

There were tire tracks beneath the snow.

They followed the trail. The tracks were deep and wide, like they came from a large SUV, a small truck, or maybe a Jeep. The track kept going for a couple hundred feet, giving rise to doubt—there was no certainty they were going to find the drug dealers' cars.

A side path to their left led to a small barn roughly eighty feet away. The tire tracks continued straight ahead on the main path.

Do they keep going or try the barn?

Sam and Ben looked at each other, mulling over their decision in silence.

"Let's have a look at the barn," Ben said, his eyes tracing the snow-covered lane. "Look, no prints or tire tracks in the snow. At least we know nobody's been this way for a while. Maybe we can crash there until this storm passes by."

"Sounds good."

Sam reached the side door. It was unlocked. The place looked conspicuously abandoned.

Inside, it was dark.

Ben closed the door behind him.

Sam fumbled with the wall, trying to find a light switch. There was a faint hum coming from the other side of the barn, suggesting the place still had usable power.

His fingers touched a dangling cord. He pulled hard and the light came on. Big compact fluorescent lights came on, taking nearly a minute to warm, before they shone brightly down on the barn's single object, like the focused lights at an antiquity exhibition.

Whatever it was, it was covered by a thick cloth.

Sam pulled it back, revealing a mint condition, 1970, second generation, cranberry red Chevrolet Camaro RS/SS underneath.

CHAPTER FORTY-SEVEN

T HE CAMARO'S STYLING was inspired by Ferrari. It was bigger and heavier than the first generation, and no longer capable of being built as a convertible. Engineered much like its predecessor, the car still used a unibody structure with a front subframe, leaf springs in the back and A-arms up front for suspension. It had the Rally Sport and the Super Sport equipment package, featuring the unique front-end appearance with a split front bumper and a center grille cavity encircled in rubber, and the heavier-duty suspension.

The red paint looked like it had just been sprayed yesterday.

The contours of the second-generation Camaro were streamlined like a racecar, with its new body style featuring a fastback roofline and ventless full-door glass with no rear side quarter windows.

Some believed it was the greatest car in Chevrolet's history. Certainly, the most powerful of the Camaros. As the years progressed, it would grow less powerful, succumbing to the pressures of tightening emissions regulations and the fuel crisis of the seventies.

Ben stared at the car, his eyes wide, and his breathing deep. "I always wanted one of these!"

"Hey, it might just be your lucky day after all," Sam said with an unsuppressed smile. "If we can get it going, you might just get to be the proud new owner of a stolen Chevrolet Camaro SS!

So much for staying inconspicuous…"

"Who cares, with a beast like this, we can outrun the police!"

Sam met him with the look of a parent about to tell a child Christmas wasn't real. Doubt was written all over his face as though he seriously doubted the classic American muscle car — albeit great for its day — could outperform a modern police car. Still, they had to work with what they had and right now, that was a nearly five decades old sports car.

"Let's see if we get can it going first."

"Okay," Ben replied. He lifted the pull-up handle and it opened smoothly. The damned thing was unlocked. "It must be our lucky day."

Sam responded with a curt, "Clearly."

"The key's sitting in the ignition! Who leaves the key in the ignition of a classic sports car?"

"Who indeed?"

Ben nodded. "Oh right, a drug dealer who knows nobody's going to be stupid enough to steal it."

"That's right. I guess he wasn't thinking about a couple of fugitives on the run."

"Guess not."

Ben reached in and pulled the hood release latch under the dash beside the steering wheel. The hood lifted a few inches with a distinctive popping sound. He eagerly moved around to the hood, reaching his fingers under to find the latch. The old coils were tight, and the hood a little stuck. He pressed down with all his weight, releasing the tension, while his forefingers depressed the latch.

The hood released.

It lifted all the way up into its self-securing hood system.

He breathed out. It was the first time he realized he was holding his breath. The 1970 Camaro SS 396 was catalogued to have a 396 cubic inch engine, that boasted a blistering 350 horsepower. It was in pristine condition, and someone had gone to the trouble of keeping the engine block warmer plugged in overnight, which dispelled any fears that the car might not still be in a drivable condition.

Whatever dilapidated state the barn might be in, there was no doubt in his mind; the owner had gone to great lengths to keep the car in perfect condition.

He turned to Sam. "Do you realize this was the first of the 1970s big block V8s?"

"No," Sam replied. "I'm afraid my dad had, how do I say this… more expensive tastes in cars when I was growing up."

"All the more shame for you."

"I guess."

"Well let me enlighten you, my friend. This was the first of the model's big block V8s and it actually displaced 402 cubic inches, although Chevrolet chose to retain the 396 badges. It's equipped with a single 4-barrel Holley carburetor that produces a staggering 375 horsepower at 5,600 rpm!"

"That's great. Really, I mean it. I get classic cars. I love them as much as the next guy, maybe even a little more. But I'm pretty certain that storm's going to hit soon, trapping us here for another day, or worse yet, those drug dealers are going to return and then it's game over — so let's just get it started and get out of here."

Ben smiled. "You bet. But I drive."

"Sure."

He unplugged the engine warmer and dropped the hood.

Outside, someone shouted, "What was that?"

Ben and Sam went silent.

Sam switched off the light.

A second voice said, "There are footprints in the snow leading to the barn!"

CHAPTER FORTY-EIGHT

B EN CLIMBED INTO the driver's seat.

He felt like an astronaut stepping into an original Apollo rocket. The car felt new, it even smelled new. But it was an anachronism. It was like driving off the car lot for the first time, nearly five decades late. The odometer displayed 865 miles. The damned car hadn't even reached its first 1000 miles. It felt like a tragedy. The car was born to be driven, not stored in pristine museum-style perpetuity.

Outside, someone fumbled with the barn's door handle.

Ben gripped the steering wheel. The curved instrument panel featured several round dials for gauges and other switches offset by a faux-wood inlay that matched the steering wheel and door panels. He ran his eyes across them. To the right were the now antique radio, cigarette lighter and ashtray at the center and glovebox door on the right.

He dipped down, hiding in the Strato bucket seats, unique to 1970 models—they featured squared-off seatbacks and adjustable headrests.

A flashlight beam shined across the car.

Someone said, "I don't see anything."

"Could it have been an animal in the snow?"

"Like what?"

"I don't know. A coyote or something?"

"I doubt it. Those weren't coyote tracks. Besides, they only reached the door. Did you see any exit tracks?"

"No." The second voice admitted, but there was impatience behind it. "Look, the barn's empty. There's nothing inside except for the old man's Camaro. Let's head back, its cold out here!"

"All right, all right." The first voice admitted. "Hang on a second, will you."

Ben heard footsteps approach.

"What is it?" the second guy asked.

"The cover isn't sitting right. If the boss came in and saw it like this, there would be hell to pay."

"So fix it and let's go."

Ben held his breath.

Beside him, Sam looked for anything that might be used as a weapon.

Ben saw the man lift the cover, fluffing it as someone would a bedsheet. He was carrying an AK47 strung casually over his shoulder and wore the vacant expression of all security guards approaching the end of the graveyard shift when nothing is happening.

Their eyes met.

The guard's eyes widened. It took a moment for incredulity to be replaced with action.

Ben didn't wait.

He turned the ignition.

The Camaro's big block V8 revved into life. Its engine produced a deep, gravelly sound, which resonated throughout the barn.

It brought a smile to Ben's face.

The guard found his composure, already trying to unsling his weapon. "Stop! Get out of the car now!"

Ben shoved his foot on the clutch, pushed the 4-speed Hurst shifter into first gear, revved the engine hard and dropped the clutch.

The tires screeched, scrambling to find their perch on the oak flooring.

The solid muscle car lurched forward, like a caged wild animal suddenly released. The car shot forward. A couple seconds later, all 3,310 pounds of steel and genuine Chevrolet craftsmanship struck the dilapidated barn door, sending the rotten wood into a mass of splintered shards.

Two shots fired!

And one of the guards shouted, "Sweet Jesus! Don't shoot the boss's car!"

Ben shifted into second.

At the end of the path he threw the steering wheel to the right, swinging the heavy car around like a go-cart.

On the main path, he kept his foot pressed down hard on the accelerator.

He jammed on the brake as they reached another fork in the road, the Camaro's tires digging into the snow-covered trail.

Ben yelled, "Which way?"

Sam gripped the edge of his seat. "Go right!"

Ben swerved to the right. A large Ford Pickup met them head on. At a glance, he could see the passenger with a machinegun ready to fire.

Ben shoved his foot on the brake and yanked the wheel round in the other direction.

"Change of plans!"

The Camaro locked its wheels, fishtailed and swung in on itself. He brought the shifter back to first. When the car completed its 180-degree slide, Ben switched from the brake to the accelerator, flooring it hard.

The tires spun in the snow before reaching the thick gravel

below, and shooting forward again.

Behind him, he heard the rapid staccato of machinegun fire.

"Don't shoot at the car!" he yelled. "Your boss won't fucking like it!"

Sam made a wry smile. "Or us for that matter!"

Ben quickly shifted up gears until the car was pummeling along a riparian trail at forty-five miles an hour. The trail snaked round two soft bends and he never once took his foot off the accelerator. He dropped down the gears as the trail dipped downward and they crossed a frozen stream, before gunning the pedal up the opposite bank.

The Camaro's engine roared in a symphony of gravelling induction noises.

Sam glanced at him and smiled.

"What?" Ben asked.

"You're enjoying this!"

"Hey, I'm entitled to! In the past seventy-two hours I've had my entire life taken away from me, everything about my life is a lie, and people keep trying to kill me — so yes, I think a little bit of fun is okay."

He reached a blind bend and threw the gear down to second.

The car slid sideways, Ben counter-locked the steering and shoved his foot down hard on the pedal. The engine cackled with pleasure.

They reached the open end of the corner and he straightened the wheel, shooting forward once more.

He turned to Sam. "All right, a LOT of fun!"

The trail dipped down into another bank, crossing a small frozen river. Half way up the next bank he jammed on the brake. In front of them, a second Ford Pickup came to a sudden stop.

Sam yelled, "Backup! Backup!"

Ben threw the shifter into reverse. He looked over his right shoulder as he headed in the opposite direction.

"Where am I going?" he asked. "Those other guys aren't that far behind us!"

"Stop!"

Ben hit the brakes.

He took in the landscape at a glance. There was a single road; it meandered around Devil's Lake — or whatever lake they were nearby. That road dipped into what would have been a shallow river crossing, but this time of year was all frozen. He had a truck in front of him and another one behind him. No way to get around either.

There was nowhere for him to go.

Sam said, "Go that way!"

Ben looked in that direction. "Are you crazy?"

More shots fired.

It was enough encouragement.

Sam yelled, "Go! Go!"

He gunned the accelerator and the Camaro lurched forward onto the icy river. It was a really bad idea. He had no idea if the surface ice would even take his weight and even if he did, it was like ice skating without the skates. The 25.5-inch original tires just didn't cut it.

The river was nearly eighty feet wide at the crossing, but it soon narrowed. Ben kept it in second gear, making the conscious decision not to use the brake.

Ben tried to steer. The wheels were getting just enough traction to still maintain control, but everything took a lot more effort. He was using bigger, stronger movements to make small corrections.

Sam glanced in the right-hand rearview mirror. "They're following!"

"All right, I guess I'll just have to speed up!"

He added just a touch more pressure to the accelerator and the Camaro rose to the challenge. The river snaked through a dense forest. Ben felt like a rally car driver, making constant changes to the steering, brake, and accelerator.

Sam glanced at him in silence, his face rigid with fear.

Ben grinned. "You know, it's not that bad. Once you accept that you never have traction and that you just have to keep adding small inputs to the controls to modify your direction, it's not that hard."

Sam gripped the dashboard. "If you say so."

The river veered to the right, sharply. A large boulder glared at them straight ahead, like impending and unforgiving doom.

Ben turned early, accelerating hard, and sending the Camaro into a sideways drift.

Ten feet from the boulder, the tires found a small amount of purchase and the car continued in the new direction.

Sam turned right around in the passenger seat. There was a loud crash behind them. It sounded like metal twisting. Sam grinned. "They didn't make it!"

"Both of them?"

"Just the first one. I don't know where the second car got to… wait!" Sam swallowed. "It's still going. One down, one to go!"

"I don't plan to let it catch up."

The river straightened and Ben increased his speed.

Sam watched him. His eyes lit up, not with fear, but with curiosity.

Ben made a slight grin. "What?"

"How are you doing this?"

"What? I'm driving a car. I've driven a car my entire adult life. What's so special about it?"

"You're driving better than most professional rally car drivers. Seriously, how are you doing this?"

Ben gave a little shrug. "Like I said when we met, I have fast reflexes. Always have."

Up ahead, the river looked like it widened again. Then Sam realized it didn't widen. It became the main lake. Ben changed down the gears quickly. It put the car into a slide. He tapped the brake and corrected, but still couldn't change his forward momentum. He was going too fast. Ben hit the brake hard, but instead of correcting the situation, the Camaro slid out coming to a complete stop nearly a hundred feet out into the lake facing back toward the ice river.

He revved the engine.

Beneath them, the ice started to creak.

His mind returned to the Camaro's 3,310-pound curb weight and wondered how much Devil's Lake could take this late in the season.

Up ahead, the driver of the Ford Pickup spotted them. Like a predator recognizing its trapped prey, he fixated on them, accelerating at full speed.

Ben waited.

In the distance, he saw the incoming driver's face alive with triumph.

When it was too late for the driver to change his mind, Ben released the brake, and took off, driving hard toward the lake's edge.

It took a second for the pickup driver to realize his mistake. In an instant, his face turned from triumph to abject fear. He tried to brake, but all it did was send the truck into an unrecoverable slide — coming to a stop just shy of the cracking ice.

The weakened ice held for a few seconds, and then, unable to support the heavier truck, finally gave way to gravity. The heavier front end was the first to fall through the ice. The occupants quickly opened the doors and jumped out. A moment later, the entire slab broke and the truck fell through.

Ben glanced at the image in his rear-view mirror and laughed. "Now I'm definitely having fun!"

He spotted a boat ramp leading to a road paved with blacktop, and took it. The road came out onto US Highway 2. Ben kicked it up to fourth and let the Camaro run free.

Next stop. Minot, North Dakota — where he would finally get answers.

CHAPTER FORTY-NINE

MINOT, NORTH DAKOTA

T HE CAMARO ENTERED the city a little before four a.m.

They approached a grain elevator ahead of them. A line of trees ran along their left, and the open fields of snow stretched all the way to the horizon on their right. They were on the outskirts of town, but somehow Sam had forgotten how sparse the place really was. It would be a stretch to say that the population was over fifty thousand. For a guy used to the East Coast, that could be a fraction of the population in a single neighborhood.

It was four a.m. exactly by the time they reached Aliana Wolfgang's house. This time of the year, the gray of dawn hadn't yet reached them, and the sky was still a velvety black. Sam made Ben park around the corner in the off chance someone predicted their destination, and then the two of them walked around the back.

It was a grand stone masonry house. The place was there for show more than purpose or pleasure. Sam had always felt it seemed like a poor fit for Aliana. She agreed. But it was her family home and after her dad died, she felt no desire to change it. Besides, sometimes she entertained large numbers of corporate guests.

Ben asked, "How long has it been since you've seen this girl?"

"A couple years," Sam replied, without missing a stride.

"Really? And you're just going to show up at her house at this time in the morning?"

"We couldn't risk tipping off your mate, Devereaux! She'll be fine. We're pretty close."

Ben arched a dark eyebrow. "So close you haven't seen her for two years... how do you know her?"

Sam turned his palms up. "We used to date for a while."

"This just gets better and better." Ben stopped walking, his cheeks creased with a well-formed grin. "Why'd you break up — and don't give me any of this 'it's complicated' crap."

"I won't," Sam met his eye. "It's not complicated. We liked each other, but our lives didn't add up. She's got a company here, I have a company that works on the oceans — just about as far from here as you can possibly get — and she didn't like the life I lead."

"And what life is that?"

"A dangerous one." Sam gave him a rueful grin. "Case in point, I've been held hostage for the past seventy-something hours."

"Hey, I said you could go more than two days ago."

Sam grinned. "See, more to the point, sometimes I can be stupid."

Ben shivered in the icy cold.

Sam said, "Come on, let's go knock on the door before we freeze to death."

He gave the door three loud knocks. Nothing gentle. Aliana was a deep sleeper — when she did make time to sleep — and he was kidding when he said they were at risk of freezing.

There was no response.

Ben looked at him and said nothing, his eyes giving him that look that said, told you, you should have called first.

Sam wouldn't have it. He knocked again, even louder.

The front porch light came on.

A moment later he heard Aliana's voice. "Good God! Sam Reilly, what the hell are you doing on my doorstep at this time in the morning?"

The door opened.

Sam looked at her, once the woman of his dreams. Their eyes met and held for a second. Sam said nothing. A sudden chill blew across his heart. She was intelligent, tall, lithe, and achingly beautiful in plaid pajamas and thick woolen dressing gown.

Sam grinned. "Would it surprise you to know that this isn't a social visit?"

Aliana sighed. "Come in, it's freezing!"

He threw his arms around her, embracing her with affection, where once there had been raw desire. She backed away after a moment.

Sam introduced Ben.

Aliana's eyes narrowed slightly, "You want to tell me what trouble you've gotten yourself into, Sam?"

"Would you believe me if I told you this time it wasn't my fault?"

She folded her hands across her lap. "No."

Over the course of the next thirty minutes and a warm cup of coffee, Sam went through what had happened, how he'd gotten there, and why he needed her help.

Aliana looked at him, her face registering a mixture of pleasure and incredulity.

Unable to take the wait any longer, Sam asked, "What are you thinking?"

"I'll need some blood. I can run a number of tests. It might take a while, but my guess is whatever made his blood so threatening is likely to show up pretty quickly."

"But?"

"No, it's nothing. You just have to realize, depending on

where the abnormality is, this could take anywhere from days to weeks. There just are so many different things to check."

Ben shook his head with a curt nod. "No, whatever it is, it showed up immediately. I mean, I donated blood and less than an hour later, I had become the prized animal at the zoo."

"All right. We can go to my lab first thing in the morning and find out."

Sam looked at her, his deep blue eyes pleading. "Any chance we could get started any earlier?"

She glanced at her watch. "It's four-thirty in the morning. Besides, have you heard the weather report? We're supposed to get the blizzard of the decade."

"We've pissed off some important people," Sam said, "There's a national manhunt for us. We don't have a lot of time."

She grabbed her keys and sighed. "All right. Let me grab my jacket. We'll take my car and go now."

On their way out, Ben glanced wistfully at the Camaro.

CHAPTER FIFTY

T OM SAID, "THAT'S Minot up ahead."
Genevieve joked, "That black smudge in the distance? How can you tell?"

Everywhere they went, everything was surrounded by a belt of trees that slowly emerged from the distance. It was hard to tell if they were looking at trees, a low thunderstorm rolling in, or even the Rocky Mountains. They weren't close enough to the mountains to see them.

Their flight had been diverted to Fargo after it became apparent that Minot was in for a devastating blizzard. Tom had hired a car and led them, arrow-like, from Fargo up to Grand Forks, then along an endless stretch of Highway 2 toward Minot. The most excitement they had was stopping for gas, and trying to figure out whether they would run out of it before they hit the next open station.

Tom put on the blinker. Out of nowhere, the rail yard had appeared outside the edge of town. He pulled up into Main Street, before finally stopping in the front of a local camping and sporting goods store. Because of the storm, it was already open, despite being just after seven a.m. People were already trying to grab survival supplies in case the weather reports being bandied about were even close to accurate.

He opened the door and stepped out of the rental car, an inconspicuous silver Ford Explorer.

The gray sky turned to pitch darkness on the horizon, where angry clouds approached.

Genevieve turned to him and said, "Let's get the supplies. We have lots of work to do before that storm hits!"

CHAPTER FIFTY-ONE

WOLFGANG RESEARCH AND DEVELOPMENT LAB, MINOT

T HE BLIZZARD HIT with speed and ferocity.

Ben recalled the evil looking, dark clouds he'd seen on their way over as the wind howled and whipped at the building's roof high above. He held his breath, wondering whether or not the building could take it. Sam sat opposite them with a mug of coffee.

Aliana applied the tourniquet to his right arm.

It seemed a lifetime ago since he first donated blood at George Washington Hospital—where all his problems had started. In fact, that was where his old life had ended and a new one commenced. He'd lost his career, the few acquaintances he might have accepted as friends, and his freedom, but hey, he'd met a few genuinely good people who had restored his faith in mankind. So, it wasn't all bad.

There was a loud bang as a tree fell on the roof. Aliana didn't flinch.

He asked, "Do you think the building will hold?"

Aliana smiled, revealing a nice set of teeth and a kindness he hadn't recognized before. "Are you kidding me?"

"No. I've survived being wrongfully imprisoned by the FBI, jumping from a helicopter shot out of the sky by my own government, a white-water rafting trip two months before the river was meant to be ridden, some drug dealers, and a whole lot of icy cold weather—so, no I'm not kidding you—I want to know, was it all for nothing because I'm about to get killed in some freak storm in North Dakota!"

She inserted the needle and started drawing blood, without breaking stride. "This building wasn't purpose built for our needs. Do you want to take a guess what its original intended purpose was?"

"No."

Sam said, "See, Aliana, it's like I said, he's no fun at all."

Ben, adequately placated said, "What was this building originally meant to be used for?"

"Storage."

"Of what?"

Aliana tilted her head slightly and grinned. "That's the right question."

"And the answer is?"

"ICBMs."

Ben's felt something large squash his chest. "Intercontinental ballistic missiles!"

"That's right," she replied calmly.

"We're sitting in a nuclear missile silo? Isn't that dangerous? Nuclear radiation or something?"

"No. ICBMs don't actually leak radiation. Besides, this one was built late during the Cold War and never put into active duty."

Ben looked at her through narrowed eyes. "You're saying Uncle Sam spent a fortune to build this place... and never used it?"

"Technically, we spent a fortune on all the nuclear silos during the Cold War and never put any of them to use. But yes, Uncle Sam paid for it, and then we got to pick it up for a song.

And now you're reaping the benefits of being inside the most secure building in Minot!"

"That's great. How long do you think the blizzard will rage?"

"They're saying it could be days, but I think they're wrong."

Ben's lips curled into a half grin. "You think the meteorologists are wrong?"

"Yep. It's like the old saying, 'weathermen and fools predict the weather.' In this, I'm betting on the fool. And why shouldn't I? I've lived here long enough to know when a storm front is moving too quickly to stay around."

"You think it will be quick?"

"Few hours at most," she replied without hesitation.

Aliana released the tourniquet and pulled out the needle. She'd withdrawn a hundred milliliters of blood into a bottle. She pressed down with her thumb hard enough that it hurt at the puncture site, and then said, "Hold this for about five minutes if you don't want to keep bleeding."

"Okay, thanks." Ben eyed the bottle of blood. It seemed like a lot. "Got enough?"

Aliana smiled. "Yeah. I wanted to get extra so that I don't have to keep poking and prodding you. One needle. Lots of blood. No repeats."

"Thanks. I appreciate it." Ben looked at her and asked, "Now what?"

"Now I'll run some tests while the storm rages on outside."

"What will that entail?"

"For the most part, I'll feed the various samples into a machine that will give me very specific answers in the format of 'yes you have something' or 'no you don't.' But I'll also put a sample under the microscope and go back to basics — see if I can spot anything unusual."

"You can do that?" Ben opened his mouth to speak and closed his eyes. "I'm sorry, what I meant to say was, people still do that sort of stuff? I thought computers spat out the readings?"

Aliana wasn't offended by his surprise. "For the most part, that's what I do. Did I mention I'm a leading geneticist? To answer your question, yes, I can look through a microscope and tell you if something's wrong—or at least different."

Sam finished his mug. He washed it in the little kitchenette and dried it with a towel, before putting it back in the cupboard. He turned to Aliana. "Don't keep us waiting. I'll bet you a romantic vacation with a guy you sometimes can stand that you'll have an answer for us two minutes after you glance at his blood."

She smiled at that. "Thanks for the vote of confidence, but it doesn't quite work like that."

"I think it does. Whatever the magic marker is that his blood contains, it was revealed almost immediately when Ben tried to donate blood. So, my guess is that you'll spot it that fast too."

"All right, but I want a trip somewhere nice and warm, like the Caribbean or Pacific Islands."

Sam said, "Agreed."

Aliana used another drawing-up needle to pull a small sample of blood from the bottle and placed it on a microscope slide. She then placed the slide on the high-powered microscope. "I hope you've got your stopwatch ticking."

Sam glanced at the clock. It was 8:20 a.m.

Aliana brought her eye up to the microscope lens, stared at the sample and then a moment later, she pushed it away again.

"I don't believe it…" she said.

"What?" Sam and Ben replied in unison.

She swallowed. "I know exactly why you were taken prisoner."

CHAPTER FIFTY-TWO

S AM ROLLED HIS eyes. "I thought you were fast, but how could you possibly know what's going on that quickly?"

Aliana sighed. "Because two days ago, I was given the identical blood sample, and asked if there was any possible way I could reproduce it."

"Come again?"

"A good friend of mine mailed it to me. She said that she'd stolen the blood after discovering the anomaly in a routine prisoner."

"Did she say why the man was a prisoner?" Ben asked.

Aliana shook her head. "No. When I asked that, she told me that prisoners had the right to blood tests as much as anyone else. It wasn't for her to go snooping into what they had done wrong to end up in prison in the first place."

Sam said, "Sure, but it's still pretty unethical. I mean, surely someone has the right to their own blood, and you can't just go around replicating it, can you?"

"Of course. That's what I told my friend once I found out. Naturally she agreed it was highly unethical, but given the anomaly, she thought it was worth breaking the law. This might just be the only case in human history."

"What was the anomaly?" Ben asked, his face crunched up in a mixture of fear and fascination.

Aliana exhaled. "Your telomeres don't shorten and yet you're still perfectly healthy."

Ben nodded. "Right, so what does that mean?"

"It means you've won the genetic lottery big time. Your blood is the Holy Grail. You're simultaneously the most valuable man alive and the most dangerous."

"Come again?" Ben asked. "Why me? What is it about me that is so valuable?"

Aliana explained what is known about telomeres, and what is still theoretical. She pointed out that not only could his genetic makeup point the way to much longer lives, but might also hold the key to preventing cancer.

Ben shrugged. "Why does this make me public enemy number one to the Department of Defense?"

"You're dangerous," Aliana insisted. "Not just because people like your genetics for its commercial value or because the government might try to hold back developments from the rest of humanity, but because if they *don't* hold back those improvements, in a couple of generations our current overpopulation problems might look like child's play."

"Really?"

"As the telomere caps shorten, they trigger the exponential process of cellular breakdown. Have you ever wondered why old people seem to be doing just fine one day, and then in a matter of years, everything starts to go bad—they have a fall, they fracture a hip, discover they have osteoporosis, and heart disease?"

"Not really," Ben replied, honestly.

Aliana ignored him and continued. "There's a trial in mice currently in which scientists have worked out how to remove the part of DNA that triggers this exponential telomere shortening. It's early days yet, but so far, they're reporting a forty percent increase in mice longevity."

"They're living longer?"

"Forty percent longer. Just imagine that in human trials."

Ben smiled. "My day just keeps on getting better."

Aliana said, "You bet it is. Do you have any idea how much time, money, and resources scientists and drug companies have spent in an attempt to unlock the secrets to lengthening telomeres?"

"I'm starting to see," Ben admitted.

"Think about it. It's the Holy Grail of human existence. Who wouldn't want to live longer, healthier, more successful lives? But in your case, we're not just talking about reducing the speeding up process, we're stopping it altogether."

"What are you saying? I'm immortal?"

"No. Technically, you're probably somewhere in the realm of a-mortal, meaning that you can die like the rest of us if you get hit by a bus or do something really stupid." Her eyes drifted toward Sam for a moment. "But every day age-related killers — heart disease, stroke, cancer — won't ever touch you."

Ben took a deep breath. "So, commercially, are you saying you can reverse engineer my blood to produce some sort of elixir of the gods that will make people live forever?"

Aliana nodded. "In theory. But that sort of research might take years to achieve. There are so many hurdles and areas that we just have no idea how it would work."

"Why? Can't you just extract whatever enzyme is in my blood and inject it into someone else?"

"Unfortunately, it doesn't work like that. There are limitations to stopping the clock."

"Like what?"

She closed her eyes, thought about it for a second. "Like Scott Kelly."

"Who?"

"He was an American astronaut with NASA."

Ben said, "Go on."

"He's an identical twin who spent 340 days in space on board the International Space Station. When he came back to Earth, they discovered that seven percent of his genes no longer matched his brother's. Space, so it would seem, alters people on a genetic level." Aliana met his eye, seeing that he was following. "Scientists discovered that Scott's telomeres — the caps at the end of chromosomes that shorten with age — stretched in space, suggesting a possible protection against ageing. It was the equivalent of turning back the internal clock by nearly two decades compared to his Earth-bound twin."

"Astronauts are effectively stopping their internal clock?" Sam asked.

"That's what everyone thought, but within two days of getting back to Earth, Scott's telomeres returned to their original length. Basically, what we see with everyone is that no matter what we do to adjust telomere length, they eventually shorten — this time faster than before."

Sam said, "Okay, so that answers the question about how they discovered Ben's unique genetic background. I just don't know why they consider him such a threat."

"I do," Aliana replied. "Of course, it's just a theory."

Sam said, "Okay, let's hear it."

"You said before that you believed Ben shares the genetic makeup of the ancient race that you've called Master Builders?"

Sam nodded. "Yeah. He has purple eyes, an eidetic memory, and lightning fast reflexes. All traits we've seen or heard about in other Master Builders."

"I thought no one had proven they ever existed?" Aliana asked.

Sam wasn't going to tell her that he had long suspected that Elise was descended from the Master Builders. "We haven't. It's still a theory, albeit a pretty strong one. I don't see them as being a different race. After all, they're almost certainly *Homo sapiens*. The difference is they have a series of genetic mutations. One being, by the sound of things, the fact that their telomeres don't shorten, meaning they live extraordinary healthy and long lives. In fact, I believe wholeheartedly that this is the reason they were able to achieve so many great feats. Imagine what you could learn and what you could do, with two lifetimes of experiences, let alone five or more?"

Ben said, "One thing I don't get. If your theory holds true, why aren't we the dominant strain? I mean, isn't that how evolution is supposed to work? If one mutation helps a lineage survive, it carries on further, and so forth?"

"I can answer that," Aliana said.

"Okay, how?"

"When I ran tests among your earlier blood samples I discovered that you have a much lower fertility rate."

Ben's face reddened. "What? I'm infertile?"

"No, you're just not as fertile as the next person. But that's okay. Think about it. If you're going to live to be a hundred and fifty, on average, then it's not as vital to pop out kids as it is for us. Replacement fertility rates are 2.1 children per human reproductive pair, at an average lifespan of 71.66 years, globally speaking. You'd need half as many children, just due to the fact that you're going to live twice as long. Only, in your case, you might live five or ten times as long. I have no idea."

They discussed the various theories throughout the storm, bandying around ideas about where to go from here and what to do, and whether or not such a genetic mutation was a blessing or a curse to humanity.

Sam discussed the labyrinth in Bolshoi Zayatsky, Russia, and that he was still waiting to hear from Tom and Genevieve about what they found there because his cell phone had died, and now Tom's phone was out of area—or perhaps, the blizzard had damaged the cellphone towers.

In the end, Sam pulled up a couch, and caught up on some much needed rest.

CHAPTER FIFTY-THREE

MINOT—5:30 P.M.

THE STORM CEASED as fast as it had erupted.

The clouds had been washed away, revealing a sky that was a hundred different shades of red, pink, blue, and deep purple. The streetlights glittered in the dusk like diamonds, catching the hard-frozen crystals on the snow.

Special Agent Ryan Devereaux breathed heavily.

This was it. He had found out that Sam and Ben were with Aliana Wolfgang at her research lab just before the blizzard took effect. He had wanted to race in and capture Ben before the storm, but it was too risky. If anything should have happened, it would have been too easy for Ben to disappear in the storm.

No, he'd made the right decision.

Now everything was set up. The blizzard had done most of the work for him, making sure to contain everything.

The Wolfgang Research and Development Lab was positioned on the u-shaped bend of the Souris River between 3rd Avenue NW and Sixth Street NW. His team had blocked off 3rd Avenue, effectively trapping them within the u-shaped bend. The river was frozen, so it could theoretically be crossed, but being in the open it was easy to guard, and with the sudden rise in water level due to the blizzard, it had made the entire river unstable and nearly impassable. This left the bridge on 3rd and 6th as the only means of escape.

Both bridges now had snow plows parked on them, making it impossible for anyone to pass.

Devereaux had no doubt his SWAT team would go in and capture him, but it was nice to know Ben was confined, even if he did slip out of the building.

He put on his flak jacket.

"All right, on my count, we storm the building…"

CHAPTER FIFTY-FOUR

S AM PICKED UP the landline in Aliana's office and called Elise.

Elise said, "Where the hell have you been? I've been trying to get through to you for hours!"

"The battery went on my phone. What's up?"

"I've reviewed the footage from the labyrinth at Bolshoi Zayatsky that Tom and Genevieve obtained."

"And?"

"Inside it was riddled with ancient texts by the Master Builders. Some of these were translated into Russian, which Genevieve could translate. But parts were missing. I've deciphered some of the Master Builder text myself. They keep referring to the Phoenix Plague. Something that will inevitably wipe out the human race, allowing a new race to rise from the ashes."

"Sounds like a theme eternal, doesn't it?"

Elise wasn't in the mood for jokes. "Sam!"

"Yes?"

"There was something else, too…" Elise's voice hardened. "We got it all wrong. We're in a lot more danger than we first thought."

CHAPTER FIFTY-FIVE

S AM LOOKED AT Ben across the room. Their eyes met and Sam held the contact just that little bit longer than what was considered normal.

Ben asked, "What is it?"

He held up the landline phone. "This is Elise, my computer hacker. She needs to talk to you."

"Me? What does your hacker want with me?"

"She's one of the smartest people you'll ever meet. I suggest you listen to what she has to say carefully."

Sam turned to Aliana. "Is there another way out of this building? Preferably one that people don't know about?"

"Yeah. There's a tunnel that runs to the building across the road. It was originally used as an escape route for the nuclear silo and was supposed to be demolished after we bought the property, but my friend inherited the company and we decided to keep the tunnel in case we ever eventually merge. It's a pharmaceutical company and we've used the tunnel on occasion to share resources when the snow blankets us in." Aliana's voice softened. "Why? What's happened?"

"That was Elise on the phone. She says there are about three hundred law enforcement officers and a SWAT team about to breach your building."

"Oh shit! All right. I'll take you downstairs, and then come back up here to try and slow them down."

"You're the best." Sam kissed her on the lips. "Ben, finish up. We've got to go!"

Ben hung up the landline. "On my way."

Sam and Ben followed Aliana to the entrance to a deep set of stairs.

"Follow this all the way to the bottom. There's a horizontal tunnel. Take it and then go up the other side. I'll call my friend. She'll help you escape."

"She doesn't even know us. Why would she help us escape?"

"I've been friends with her since college. I'd trust her with my life."

Sam took a deep breath. "And now we're trusting her with ours."

"All right," confirmed Ben.

Sam and Ben ran down the series of steep spiral stairs, taking two to three steps at a time. The bottom opened to a horizontal tunnel. They raced across it and then climbed the stairs at the opposite end that mirrored the ones they had descended.

At the top of the stairs they were greeted by Aliana's friend.

She was a petite blonde woman who looked very young, with pretty blue eyes, dimples, and a soft, sweet voice. "Quick, this way."

Sam nodded a curt, "Thank you."

He and Ben followed her at a brisk walk.

In her office, she swiped her ID card and waited for the elevator. Sam swept her office with his eyes, surprised to see the layout was almost identical to Aliana's. His gaze landed on a collection of picture frames on a desk.

One of them took his breath away. It was a picture of an older man, standing beside a red Chevrolet Camaro. Sam knew at a glance, that it was a second generation, RS/SS. He knew this, of course, because he'd been in that very car earlier that morning.

She noticed his interest in the car and smiled. She had a cute, almost impish smile that teased of fun that any man would want to explore.

"You like the car?" she asked.

"Yeah," Sam replied. "It's a thing of beauty."

"And a blast to drive. That's my father. He used to love that car. I keep it these days, stored for safe keeping, out of respect and nostalgia."

"I'm sorry to hear about your father."

"Don't be," she replied. "It was a long time ago. He was unwell. There was nothing anyone could do. I took over his business and have been managing his family enterprise ever since."

Ben stared at her. "Have we met before?"

Sam eyes flashed a warning.

But Ben ignored it. "No. I do remember you. It's your smile, you see. I would never forget your smile. Even if you injected me with a sedative and an amnesic the last time we met. What was your name? Emma! That's right!"

The elevator door opened with a beep.

Emma levelled a Berretta M9 handgun at them both. "Yes. That would be me. I've seen how fast you move. Now stand over there."

Ben shuffled backward.

Sam looked at her. "What do you want?"

"The same thing everyone wants – to live forever – and, so long as we're asking, I'd like to become filthy rich."

"Is that why you turned to producing methamphetamines?" Sam asked.

She took an audible gasp, her face suddenly pale. "What do you know about that?" She shrugged. "If you must know, that one I didn't do for riches. That one I did out of desperation. My father died, and I inherited his legitimate business, which was about to go bankrupt. I mean, how does someone screw up pharmaceuticals in America?"

Sam said, "Indeed?"

"And I needed his business to stay afloat, long enough for me to change the world."

Sam stared at her with piercing blue eyes. "You want to cure cancer?"

"I do."

"Is that why you sent a team of mercenaries to Bolshoi Zayatsky to stop my friends finding out the truth?"

She smiled, shook her head, denying it, but without any real enthusiasm. "I'm afraid I never liked spy movies and I don't have time for soliloquies... Ben, you're coming with me, Sam... Goodbye."

Sam looked at her, fear and disbelief written on his hardened face.

She shifted her hand, aimed the Berretta at his chest and squeezed the trigger.

Bang!

CHAPTER FIFTY-SIX

BEN DIVED AT Emma.

The forced knocked her over. Still gripping the handgun, she tried to turn it on him, but she was no match for his speed.

He disarmed her in one movement.

She put her palms skyward. "I'm sorry. You don't understand what's at stake here. You don't understand what THEY will do to me if I don't get you back."

"Who are THEY?

"No. I can't say, they will kill me."

Ben pointed the handgun at her. "If you don't say, I will kill you!"

She shrugged. "Some things are bigger than you, bigger than me. Some things are worth sacrificing everything for."

"Emma! Who's behind this!"

She pulled a flick knife out and lunged at him.

Ben squeezed the trigger, and released three rounds before she got anywhere near him. He shook his head, looking at her once beautiful body, now horribly distorted in death. She never even stood a chance.

Ben turned to Sam. "You okay?"

He clutched his chest. Blood dribbled out a single gunshot wound to the right side of his chest. He coughed. There was a fine mist of blood in his mouth. "I'm not going to lie to you, this hurts like hell!"

Ben said, "Sweet Jesus, you've been shot! We need to get you to the hospital."

"No. We need to get you out. It's your life that counts now."

Ben rolled Emma over, taking her ID swipe card and her keys to her car — a Porsche Cayenne. "Time to go. Can you walk?"

Sam nodded. "I'll be fine."

He stood up, but couldn't stay up.

Ben put his arm under Sam's left shoulder and helped him into the elevator. He hit the button for the carpark.

Outside, Ben found her car parked closest to the elevator.

He clicked the remote button and opened the door to slide Sam in. Next to him, Sam's breathing was getting faster.

"You okay? Can you breathe?"

"I'll live," Sam said. "Go!"

Ben turned the ignition key and the V8 Turbo roared. He released the electronic handbrake and drove down the series of downward spiralling ramps.

At the bottom, he pulled onto Cortland Drive, and then turned right onto 8th Street. The Porsche SUV hugged the snow-covered road like a tractor on steroids. He flicked the paddles behind the steering wheel and changed down gears again, turning left onto 4th. He gunned the accelerator and raced forward. When he reached 6th Street he shoved his foot on the brake.

The Porsche fishtailed on the ice, until its ABS anti-skid system managed to determine the most successful means of bringing the heavy SUV to a stop.

Ben stared at the array of police cars, blocking his escape route by every means. His heart pounded in the back of his head and he felt fear stir in his throat like bile. At the end of the bridge, a single snow plow blocked his only means across the Souris River and out of the trap.

Sam looked at him. "What?"

Ben said, "We've had a good run, Sam. I want to thank you for everything you've done for me. But we both know it's time for you to get out."

Sam laughed. "You don't want me to come?"

"You know what has to happen from here. This isn't Thelma and Louise—hell, I still don't know if I like you. Either way, there's no reason for you to follow me to the end."

Sam gave him his hand. "You're okay, Ben."

Ben took it with a firm shake. "Yeah, you too. Thanks for everything."

Sam swallowed hard. "Good luck."

Sam stepped out of the car, collapsing on the icy road. Behind him, an ambulance raced to greet him.

Ben revved the powerful V8 Turbo.

He released the brake and the Porsche leapt into an eager gallop.

CHAPTER FIFTY-SEVEN

S PECIAL AGENT RYAN Devereaux stood at the bridge on 6th Street. His eyes squinted as he fixed his gaze on the black SUV.

"What the hell's he trying to do?" He levelled his eyes directly at him. "Doesn't Ben know he's surrounded? There's no way out of this alive."

The Secretary of Defense stood next to Devereaux. "There's no way out of this for him even if he comes willingly."

He met her gaze through narrowed eyes. "Everyone should be given a chance."

"Not Ben. You know what's at stake."

"Yes, ma'am."

The Porsche picked up speed, racing straight for the bridge.

Devereaux and the Secretary of Defense stepped back.

The Porsche shot toward the bridge.

It was an exercise in futility. With the snow plow parked in the middle of the bridge, there was no way he could get across it. And everywhere else was thick snow. There was only one way in and one way out of the area.

It was Ben's own personal labyrinth.

The SUV swerved at the last moment, breaking through the railing and driving off the side of the bridge.

It launched into the air, and crashed through the thin layer of ice into the flowing water beneath.

Devereaux and the Secretary of Defense ran to the edge of the bridge.

The water was flowing fast beneath the ice. They watched as the car drifted down the river, far below the ice. It might take weeks to locate the car. One thing was certain: no one could survive that.

Ben Gellie was dead.

CHAPTER FIFTY-EIGHT

THE SECRETARY OF Defense came up to greet Sam in the back of the ambulance.

Aliana Wolfgang was sitting with him, too. She stood up, immediately and greeted her, "Madam Secretary. I'll leave you two to talk in private." Aliana turned to Sam. "When you get better, you still owe me a vacation somewhere."

Sam grinned. "Agreed."

The Secretary of Defense turned to him, "How do you feel?"

"Well, I got shot, and then my lung collapsed so these fine paramedics," his eyes drifted toward the two paramedics, "Shona and Danny stuck a needle in my chest to reinflate my lung. Apart from that, I'm pretty good."

"Good man."

Sam closed his eyes. When he opened them again, he looked like he'd just remembered what he was doing there, his mind flashing back to Ben Gellie. He turned his head to face her. "Is he dead?"

She nodded. "Yes. It's over."

"Thank goodness." He took a deep breath—it looked painful as all hell—and then sighed. "You know we killed the wrong man, don't you?"

Her eyes narrowed. "What the hell are you saying?"

"Genevieve and Tom went to the labyrinth at Bolshoi

Zayatsky."

"And? What did they find?" Her voice, now a whisper.

"Someone has redacted the important parts of the ancient Master Builder text within the labyrinth — the Russian parts that is — no one at the time knew how to decipher the ancient script of the Master Builders."

"John and Jenny Gellie weren't developing the Phoenix Plague?"

He shook his head. "No. They were trying to develop a genetic solution. Ben Gellie was meant to be the genetic antidote to the Phoenix Plague."

"And we got him killed!"

Sam raised his voice, "Someone set this up. This wasn't an accident. It was a targeted attack, spanning back to the seventies, when the Department of Defense first got involved in the investigation of the Bolshoi Zayatsky labyrinth."

"Everything about the original team has been redacted. There's no record of the original investigators," the Secretary concluded grimly.

Sam said, "The Phoenix Plague is still out there, and someone just succeeded in destroying the only antidote ever developed."

"I know."

"You know what that means?"

"Yes. We have a traitor among us."

CHAPTER FIFTY-NINE

S AM MUST HAVE blanked out for a minute or two.

When he woke up, Special Agent Ryan Devereaux was waiting for him.

He blinked. "You must be Devereaux."

"Yes, sir."

"Do you mind if I go to the hospital before you take my statement? I'm a little tired."

"I'm not here to take your statement, Mr. Reilly."

Sam blinked again, trying to stay awake. "You're not?"

"No. I just wanted to apologize for ever doubting you, sir. I thought..." Devereaux's eyes dipped downward. "I thought you might have been working with Ben Gellie. I see I was wrong."

Sam gave him a curt nod. "It's okay. You could only work with what you had."

"I did wonder, though..."

"What?"

"How a man without military training could keep you captive all this time... what with us finding my original service issued Glock at the helicopter wreck site, and all."

"Good question. As you know, things don't always add up." Sam grinned. "On that subject, there's a woman named Emma Thompson. I believe she was one of your doctors. She inherited a pharmaceuticals company. If you look into her land holdings around the place, I think you might find quite a syndicate of meth labs."

"Really?"

Sam nodded. "Yeah. We came across one about ten miles south of Devil's Lake."

"All right. We'll take a look. Thank you."

Devereaux stood up to leave.

Sam said, "Best of luck."

The Secretary of Defense stepped back into the ambulance. "Sorry about that. He was feeling guilty."

Sam shrugged, as best he could with his injuries. "What the hell do you care about his feelings?"

"I don't." She made a wry smile. "Hell, I don't even care about your feelings—just so long as you get better, and get back to work."

"So what are you doing here?"

"I forgot to show you something."

Sam shuffled back in the ambulance stretcher, uncomfortably. "What?"

"Three months ago you discovered what you thought might have been the wreckage of Amelia Earhart's Electra... there was no sign of her or her navigator Fred Noonan's remains, but you did find an antique camera."

Sam nodded. "Go on."

"Our Historical Photographs Department developed the photos. I thought you might want to see one in particular."

Sam felt his heart race. "For goodness sake, go on!"

"I should warn you, we couldn't establish whether or not the photos were indeed taken by Ms. Earhart." The Secretary smiled and handed him a duplicate of the photo. "But I thought you might find this one just as interesting."

Sam stared at the photograph.

It depicted a cave. It had a unique purple hue to it. A crepuscular beam shined down on the polished rockface making it stand out like a prized painting at a museum exhibition.

He focused on the pictograms etched into the rockface. The photo's resolution wasn't good enough to make out the intricate details, but there was no doubt about the basic design. Each one depicted a human face.

There were seven in total.

The faces, clearly the same prehistoric hominids from Ben's photo, adorned the same cave wall.

Sam handed it back to the Secretary of Defense.

He had seen a similar photo before. Obviously, it wasn't the same photo, but it was the same location. It was the same place in which the Ben Gellie's only family photo had been taken.

CHAPTER SIXTY

BEN GELLIE HUDDLED by a fire in an abandoned, half-collapsed old red barn nearly a mile east of where he'd crashed into the Souris River.

His hair had finished drying.

Next to him lay his face mask and SCUBA tanks. If Genevieve and Tom had not acted when they did, he would have died of hypothermia well before he drowned.

As it was, he owed them his life.

Elise walked into the barn.

His eyes lit up and he embraced her with a tender hug.

Ben smiled and gave her a hug. "Hello, my sister… you've grown since I last saw you."

"Hello Ben. I wish I could remember you. I was crawling last time I saw you. But I remember your voice. I knew for certain the second I spoke with you on the phone."

She handed him a new passport, social security number, bank details, and educational records.

"All fake?" he asked.

"No. All legitimate. I hacked into the various governing bodies that look after each field. Everything you see will stand up to any examination someone might attempt. Oh, and by the way, I put a couple million dollars in your account. No reason you should be poor in your new life."

"Thank you. I wish there was more that I could do for you." He embraced her again. "And I wish I could spend more time with you."

"One day. All of this will be behind us, and we can be together as a family."

He wore his heart in his throat. "Do you know what happened to our parents?"

"No. But I intend to find out," she replied.

He picked up his small bag of new belongings. "I should go."

"You know how to contact me?"

"Yes."

Her eyes welled. "Where will you go?"

"I've always wanted to do some traveling along the west coast, but have never found the time. Maybe I'll make that time now… do some sightseeing."

Elise grinned. "Oh, that reminds me. Here are the keys. You'll be happy to know it's now legally registered in your new name with a brand new set of license plates."

Ben looked at the keys and smiled. "I've always wanted to own a Chevrolet Camaro RS/SS. This must be my lucky day."

"Good bye, Ben. Remember, you're not alone. You have a family who loves you very much."

"I know."

He stepped out of the barn and climbed into the cranberry red sports car of his dreams. Nearly fifty years old, and just like him, it was about to really live life for the first time. He started the engine, put it into gear, and headed out west on Highway 2.

THE END

WANT MORE?

Join my email list and get a FREE and EXCLUSIVE Sam Reilly story that's not available anywhere else!
Join here ~ www.bit.ly/ChristopherCartwright

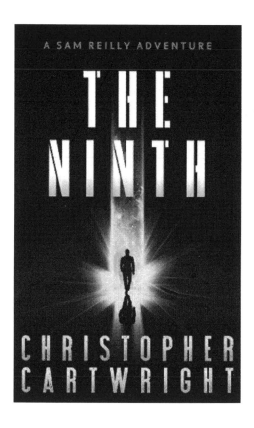

Printed in Great Britain
by Amazon